The
Black Bridge Road

A Midwestern boy's experiences growing up
somewhere between the city and the country

Don Allison

Illustrations by the author

THE BLACK BRIDGE ROAD

First edition. December 10, 2022.

Copyright © 2022 Don Allison.

ISBN: 978-0974000251

Written by Don Allison.

Also by Don Allison

Charlie
The Black Bridge Road

Table of Contents

Dedicated to friendships that have lasted...
and those I wish had.

Times are bad. Children no longer obey their parents, and everyone is writing a book."
Marcus Tullius Cicero (106-43 BC)

Acknowledgements

Writing this book had long been a dream of mine. And while I had completed many of these stories, I procrastinated, allowing other things to push completion aside. But then I received a Christmas card from "Schultzie," a character in this book. In it, he wrote only, "Where's the book?" That was the last straw! I had to do something, and there were only two things I could do; finish the book or move.

So, to Ron Schultz, "Schultzie," I say thank you. Your card still holds a prominent place on my bulletin board, reminding me of your encouragement, of the years we spent together trying to grow up, and now the completion of that dream.

I wish I could thank my high school English teacher, Mrs. Nichols. But I fear I am too late. She was the only teacher who, after reading my blundering attempts at essays and speeches, somehow saw enough in me, the class clown, to encourage me to do more. My failure to thank her in time is another example of my procrastination. Don't you do it too.

And I need to thank a wonderful old friend of mine, George Bachay, who encouraged me in many ways. George told me how he once sat watching a movie on television with his wife and he complained about it saying, "I can write that good." So, she challenged him by saying, "Well, why don't you then?" And he did. Likewise, George challenged me to follow suit.

Finally, I want to thank my wife, my best friend, and my girlfriend. They are the same, by the way. Lyn has been very patient and supportive of me all these many years. She has heard these stories many times and has provided much needed criticism. Without a doubt, I have tried her patience.

Introduction

I was driving the wooded backroads of the Meteor Hills country in northwest Wisconsin, looking for my Uncle Freeman's farm. I hadn't seen it since his passing. When I was a boy, his log cabin stood amid the trees of the surrounding forest. If you didn't know where to look, you might never see it.

A small stream ran past the house, clear and cold, falling into small dark pools. Mayflies danced while minnows darted to and fro. I longed to visit this place of my childhood once more.

I thought of my family's infrequent visits, remembering the long gravel drive leading to his farmhouse, and the smells of the milking barn at the top of the hill. I remembered the fragrance of warm hay stacked high, and of course, manure.

As I drove, the aroma of damp vegetation reminded me of the moss that grew in the shade of the stream, and I wondered if I might again see the things I had once known.

I thought how my cousin Sammy dared me to ride a cow, and how we once spent the night in a makeshift tent beside the brook where I lay thinking what a wonderful, peaceful place this was – until a Canada lynx screamed in the night. It's sound pierced the darkness like a woman screaming in terror. It terrified me anyway.

Nearing the turnoff, I recalled sitting on the massive concrete steps in front of Uncle Freeman's home, soaking in the sunshine and, looking behind me, seeing a large pine snake, sharing the porch and the sun with me.

Many memories rushed to my mind, and now I was going back for a long overdue visit. The road was gravel then. Now it's blacktop. The land has changed little, still densely wooded with occasional small fields and pastures.

I recognized the turnoff where a garage-size boulder stood as a landmark. I turned. The lane seemed familiar yet was very different. It was weedy and overgrown with brush. The stream, once clear and rocky, was shallow and a murky brown. I had never seen it that way before, not even after a heavy rain.

Driving further down the lane, brush crowded closer, and ruts gave way to grass. The path ended where a tree had fallen across it. Ahead, the lane was little more than an allusion, nearly reclaimed by the forest.

I might have walked the rest of the way, but I couldn't force myself to do it. Too much had changed. I was afraid of what I might find – or lose. Besides, I knew I wouldn't find what I was really looking for. And to try would only destroy what I still held. And I'd rather keep that alive – if only in my memory.

As I returned home, I thought more about the days of my youth. Memories flooded my mind. It was then that I decided there had to be a way to preserve those precious days, to share with others what life was like, and what it could be again, if people cared. And so, this book.

For some people, reaching their destination is their goal. For others, it is the journey that matters. If you are one of the latter, you will enjoy these stories. My objective has been to transport you back in time, if not in reality, then in your mind.

Herein then is a collection of stories about a boy growing up, about life as it was, about freedom and friendships and innocence. Not everything was good, of course, but it was real, just as these stories are real. Some of the names have been changed while others have not. That may be to protect the people in the stories or confuse you. Or it may be to protect me. Which is which is for you to wonder about.

Some of the events may have occurred in a different order than I relate them. That I have taken liberty to move things about is not important. What is important is that I captured the essence of the era when this country had risen from the depths of war to its zenith. And zenith it was, I fear, for history will surely prove that the times of which I write were truly the best this nation will ever know, and try as we might, we can never go back.

Chapter 1
Old John

M any of us are suspicious of strangers, perhaps all of us are, but for the very young, for they have not yet learned to be prejudiced. But once we become aware of the differences in others, our fears and imaginations can take us to extremes.

Through our kitchen window, I could see the small shack where the old man lived. I was aware of his "mysterious" appearances and disappearances. I saw that his life was different from my own, therefore, I feared Old John.

A vast sandpit a half-mile from my home was keenly important to me when I was a boy. At the far end of the pit, the Janesville Sand and Gravel Company manufactured concrete blocks. The blocks they produced contained rocks of many shapes and colors, some with fossils and other evidence of life long past. Some may also have held evidence of another kind.

John was a neighbor of mine, a sailor in the merchant marine. Having traveled the world over many times, he was home no more than twice a year. When he was, we saw him only briefly.

He lived in a tarpaper-covered shack on a weedy, overgrown lot behind my family's home. He didn't need to live in the shack for he wasn't poor. Not that poor, anyway. He owned a house on the lot adjoining his shack, but he rented the house to others because he was away so much of the time.

His shack measured little more than ten by fifteen feet. It had one door, no windows, and no running water. A single bare light bulb hung from the ceiling providing light. Thick brush and tall weeds filled his yard like a jungle. A small, weed-filled garden once grew along one side of his yard, and a tall wire fence surrounded the whole of it.

We knew very little about John. He had no family that we knew of. He didn't talk, certainly not to us kids anyway. His comings and goings were a puzzle to us. He was strange and mysterious, someone to make fun of, someone to fear.

When John was home from the sea, he spent much of his time at Slick's, a neighborhood tavern. Although he seemed like an unfriendly man to us, John sometimes talked with the other neighborhood men who stopped in at Slick's, perhaps even to my father, though if he did, I never heard about it. We often saw John as he left the tavern, carting with him a case of beer in a wheelbarrow. With this treasure, he went back to his shack where he continued drinking alone.

One day my friends Bud and Schultzie and I sat at a table inside Chet's, the local soda shop, across the road from Slick's. We were discussing the day's events when, through the window, we saw John leave Slick's. Wearing his usual blue denim jacket and pants, and a Greek fisherman's cap, he appeared to be headed home, as usual, hauling a case of beer. Curious about this mysterious man, we talked about how it would be a great adventure to see inside his shack, to learn more about him. We wondered how he lived, what he did, where he traveled, and what he was really like.

We had heard so many stories about him. Perhaps he was a spy, we imagined, maybe even a killer. We convinced ourselves it would be best for everyone if we discovered more about him. So, we talked and planned, then justified our plans through his being so alien. The best interest of the neighborhood would be served, we told ourselves, if we exposed his many dark secrets. We felt obligated to learn more about him, and so we agreed that breaking into his home was not a crime. In fact, it was our certain duty.

So, late one hot summer evening, shortly after Old John had returned to the sea, Bud, Schultzie and I met to carry out our plan. The neighborhood was alive with activity, the evening being too hot for sleeping. Some neighbors sat on their porches visiting, and some were strolling together. Others had invited friends over to play cards. The three of us walked around the block several times until we learned where everyone was. Then we made our move.

Homes surrounded John's fenced-in lot, so we had to be careful not to be seen or heard. No streetlights lit our neighborhood, making darkness our ally. Finally, the time was right. We ducked into some bushes beside his fence. The neighbors who rented John's house were still up. Their lights were on and their windows open, not forty feet away from John's shack. These neighbors might easily hear us if we weren't careful. We dared make no noise.

Taking a flashlight and screwdriver, we sneaked beneath the fence and slinked through the dense weeds. Quietly, Schultzie placed the screwdriver between the door and the jamb and pried. Almost too easily, the door opened. We crept in. Once inside, I shut the door. Bud turned on the flashlight and there before us was everything we needed to tell us about Old John.

The room was cluttered, to say the least. Every surface had something on it. His cot, a chair, a bench that served as a table, and the floor, all were covered with various items and pieces of "evidence." We saw beer bottles of course, and newspapers, matches and cigarettes from every country of the globe; there were dirty clothes and money. Money! Coins from around the world lay scattered everywhere. Some in cups, some in boxes, others with holes in them or with odd shapes. There were words in strange languages, figures I'd never seen before, and metals unlike any coins I had ever known.

Each of us gathered different bits of this "evidence" to show that John was a spy for some distant nation. I filled my pockets with coins. Bud took several packs of cigarettes. What Schultzie took, if anything, I don't know, for we heard a noise outside.

Our flashlight was out in a moment. Our hearts beat loudly. I held my breath. We sweated from more than just the heat. A whispered warning from Bud was all we needed, "Let's get outa here!" he said.

Standing nearest the door, I reached for it, but something pushed me hard. The door flung open, and footsteps pounded through the brush. I gasped for breath and fumbled to regain my balance. I heard someone crash against the fence. Darting out the door, I tripped on a rock and fell. The fence squeaked as someone climbed over. Excited voices whispered loudly. Then I heard the sound of footsteps running down the road.

I picked myself up and looked around. Bud and Schultzie were gone. It was they who had pushed past me in their hurry to get out the door. It was they who ran through the brush and climbed the fence. It was their excited voices and their footsteps I had heard. I listened. I heard nothing more. I waited.

What was it we had heard? What was it that had frightened us? Then I heard voices from the house next door. I heard glasses clink and laughter. The people there were playing cards around the kitchen table and had not heard us.

Slowly, I crept in darkness through the weeds and brush. I was still frightened. Where, I wondered had Bud and Schultzie gone? What was it we had heard? I sneaked beneath the fence near the road concealing brush. Minutes passed, yet I waited. I was too frightened to know if I should run, exposing myself, or if I should stay hidden. Then I wondered is it possible that someone else was in the brush watching me.

I heard footsteps. Someone was coming along the dark road. Faintly, I made out the dark forms of two people. They slowed when near me and whispered together, looking toward the fence. It was Bud and Schultzie. They had come back to see what had happened to me.

They couldn't see me, hidden in the brush and began to walk away. I hoarsely whispered, "Hey, guys!" They stopped. I ran out to join them, and together we hurried away sharing our excitement.

We never told anyone of our adventure, nor of the "evidence" we had gathered. We decided it was best to keep it against the time when it might be called for. I had several coins, many coins, in fact, forty or fifty of them. They had little monetary value, but to me they were priceless, like medals won on a heroic adventure. And in a sense, they were. They also became a greater source of wonder to me, of distant lands and people, and they caused me to wonder more about John and his many travels and encounters.

THAT NEXT SPRING, JOHN returned. Several times, from our back steps, I watched him go in and out of his shack. He had been to the neighborhood tavern of course, perhaps telling the men there that someone had been in his shack. Maybe there would be an investigation, I thought. Maybe someone had seen the three of us there that night.

Schultzie was away for the summer, and Bud had smoked what evidence he had. But I still had the coins. Guilt and worry crept in about me. I was afraid I might be found with the coins and questions would be asked. Authorities might ask how I got them. I was afraid I might be linked to Old John, either as a fellow spy, or as someone who had broken into his shack. Either way I saw nothing but trouble. I decided to get rid of the coins. But, where, I wondered. How? Then it came to me. The perfect place. The sand pit.

I gathered the coins from their hiding place under a loose board in my bedroom closet and put them in my pockets. Then I walked down the Black Bridge Road to the sandpit where, one-by-one, I threw them over the steep edge of the pit, gone forever. Or were they?

ONE AFTERNOON, JOHN stepped from the tavern and started across the highway toward Chet's. Those who saw it said he failed to look and simply walked into the path of an oncoming fuel truck. He died there, alone. His mysterious life ended in a moment.

I often wished I had kept those coins, or at least one of them anyway. I have since wondered how many of them were cast into the concrete blocks made by Janesville Sand and Gravel Company. How many had been found by those working there or by builders using the blocks? What might someone have thought upon finding a coin from some distant country cast into one? How many mysteries might others have conjured up by the strange appearance of those coins? One can only wonder.

Chapter 2
Arrival

While our nation was striving to recover from the Great Depression, jobs were scarce. To work, to eat, to have any chance for a home of their own, many people were forced to move, my parents among them.

Arriving from northern Wisconsin they found many others like them, young families mostly, people from diverse backgrounds. But all had one thing in common, a strong work ethic and the instinct to survive.

Our home was a walk-in freezer. At least, it was originally. Before I was born, my father purchased the freezer from a local business that had closed, and after dismantling it, used the materials to erect a simple one-room home on the outskirts of town.

Jobs and money were scarce, and people like my parents had to do what they could to get by. My folks had grown up in northern Wisconsin where the timber industry, once such a vital force, was dying. The failure of Big Timber made survival difficult for many related businesses, railroading, grocery, clothing, and others. Farmers too, barely eked out a living on the poor soils of the north. Even taverns, among the first to come and last to go, struggled.

Shortly after marrying, my parents moved to Janesville bringing with them an infant son, my brother Kenneth. I wasn't due to come along for another ten years. Families were quick to help each other in those days, more than they are today, so for a while my parents lived with mother's relatives.

My father found work in a tobacco warehouse where he earned forty cents an hour and somehow managed to save twenty dollars, ten for the down payment on the walk-in freezer and another ten dollars for down payment on a small lot. By then, a second son, my brother Chuck, was born.

The lot my father bought had a partially dug basement and a foundation of concrete blocks, remnants of the previous owner's attempt to build his home. Unable to pay what he owed during the Great Depression; the property was lost to the bank. Over the following years, neighbors used the vacant lot as a dump, nearly filling it with trash.

Clearing away the trash, Dad erected our one-room home, covering it with tarpaper and dividing it into two rooms with a canvas partition. Then he turned to his next problem, water.

People today think nothing of going to the kitchen and turning on a tap to get water, hot or cold, in abundance. But we didn't have running water and Dad could not afford to drill a well. Nearly everyone in our neighborhood got their drinking water from a community well. We kept our drinking water in a galvanized metal pail just inside the back door, and our whole family drank from the same long-handled dipper that hung from the side of the pail.

Usually, it was the children's job to take their coaster wagon or to carry a pail to the well for water each day. Hanging the pail from a lip on the pump, we grasped the handle and pumped until cold, clear water poured forth. We were careful not to spill too much on the way home for the longer the water lasted the longer it was before we had to repeat the trip.

However, one could hardly carry enough water home for washing clothes or bathing. For that, we used rainwater. A downspout funneled rain from our roof into a storage cistern.

With little more than a shovel and his sweat, Dad dug a cistern fifteen feet deep and seven feet across, lining it with brick and mortar.

As it grew deeper, Mom stood above and pulled pails of dirt and gravel up, dumping it in a pile. Tossing the pail back down, it was filled again and again.

Dad often told how Mom once tossed the pail down to him when he wasn't looking, striking him squarely on the head. Surprised and angry words floated up from the depths of that pit, only to be drowned out by mother's laughter.

In the summer of 1941, my folks partitioned their single room home, adding a bedroom and a kitchen. They had just finished the addition in September when a baby girl, my sister Karen was born.

That following winter, Dad completed digging the basement. And just as with the cistern, Mom hauled the dirt out by rope and bucket, while

Dad dug beneath the house, shoring up the footings with concrete blocks as he progressed. Ever so slowly, the basement was made ready for the coal furnace to be installed the following spring.

Building the house first and then the basement was in reverse to how a home should be built, but they had little choice. A place to live had been their first priority.

When World War II broke out, my father got a job as a forger at Fairbanks-Morse in Beloit. There he made nearly $100 a week, far more than the $16 he had been making. When the next summer came, with the war still raging, he found a job making ammunition at General Motors.

After the war ended, he was again without a job, but with the money he had saved, he built a second story to their home. The new addition included an indoor bathroom which required a septic system. No longer could they simply throw the water out the back door. So again, the shovel and pail were brought out.

Life was difficult, not just for my folks, but for nearly everyone. My folks worked hard, sure. They expected to work hard. But maybe the hardships they had to endure were preparing them for what was to come. Me.

Chapter 3
Cause for Celebration

When people say they remember little about their childhood, I wonder, how can they not remember at least something? Did nothing significant happen to them? Have they taken life for granted? And what explains my remembering so much?

The day I was born there was dancing in the streets. Not just in my neighborhood, not just in Janesville, but throughout the United States. It was a wonderful welcome, I thought, though later I found it wasn't for me they were dancing. It was for the end of World War II, for I was born on Thursday, August 9, 1945, the day the United States dropped the second atomic bomb on the Japanese. Bitterly disappointed, I left the hospital with my mother and went home to cry about it for weeks.

I don't really remember the end of the war, but I do remember many things from very early in life, like awakening early one morning with a sense of impending danger. Something terrible was about to happen. A pale-yellow light crept around the edge of the window shade, lighting the curtains as night dissolved into dawn. I strained to identify the two forms lying motionless on a bed nearby. My eyes scanned the darkened room. I could scarcely identify a ceiling light and a picture on the wall. Dark shapes loomed on the dresser.

I couldn't get up. I tried to cry out, to make some sort of noise, to warn others in the house of the danger I felt, but I couldn't speak. As my eyes darted about the room, I felt the danger grow more urgent. Vertical bars separated me from the others. I struggled. Then suddenly, with a crash, my crib collapsed, sending me and my mattress and blankets sprawling onto the floor where I lay crying until Mom picked me up and placed me in bed with her and Dad.

YET ANOTHER MEMORY finds me sitting in a metal stroller in our living room. The stroller was blue and white in color and had a wooden handlebar and a toy tray in the front with various colored beads on a rod that I could push from side to side. A removable handle and foot-tray converted the stroller into a walker.

One day, while sitting quietly in my walker in our living room, I looked up and saw my mother and another woman in the kitchen. Next to them was another creature – a baby just like me. I had never seen another baby before.

It turned out that baby was my cousin, Judy. She was three months younger than I and Mom, and my Aunt Bertha were changing her diaper. Judy and I were to become fast friends while growing up, sharing many adventures on the lakes of northern Wisconsin where her family eventually moved.

BATH-TIME WAS A SIGNIFICANT experience for me as a toddler. I still remember those baths with a clarity that makes me blush. Our family had no bathinette, so Mom bathed me in the kitchen sink where I was lathered and rinsed, then made to stand naked in front of the kitchen window where I was toweled off. I hated those baths with the cold porcelain sink on my bottom and the whole world outside the window watching me. Even at that early age, I felt embarrassed.

Some people may doubt my remembering anything from such an early age, but significant events are impressed deeply into one's mind. So much of the world was a wonder that, to me, many things were memorable.

One such event occurred when I was a toddler carried by my grandmother along the Yahara River. On a 4-H club picnic with my parents and some of our neighbors, we followed a wooded path beside this sparkling stream. The river was shallow where it passed through the park. Dark shadows fell across the water from dense trees on either side of the river while birds sang, and voices rang from children playing tag.

We heard splashing on the far side of the stream, and I heard excitement in Dad's voice as he said, "Garfish!" Then he and some others quickly searched the woods for sticks to use as clubs, then waded into the water to do battle.

I vividly remember the splashing and thrashing as they clubbed and slashed at the fish, trying to kill as many as they could, and the anger in my father's voice later as he spoke of what he called, "those primitive and worthless fish."

Years later, I asked him about that incident, and he marveled that I might remember it since I was so young. But, because it was significant to me, it burned itself into my memory, like my first venture away from home alone.

That time I took along a sense of awe and wonder, and little else. Alone, in rubber pants and T-shirt, I walked down the middle of what was then Logan Street, past familiar looking homes of families I would grow to know, Arndt, and Mathews on my right, Hoff, McNamee and Kelly on my left.

My mother didn't know I had left the yard as I walked, looking left and right, gaping in wonder at the vastness of this newfound world. I noticed people working in their gardens and birds chirping in the swaying limbs of trees overhead. I came to the community water pump, taking in all that was around, discovering for the first time the sights and sounds of summer – and freedom.

Passing the community well, I turned the corner and continued on Witt Street where I was captivated by the beauty of the expanse opening up before me.

Suddenly a giggling, red-haired girl, named Sandy, ran up behind me. This was my first encounter with the opposite sex, and I was not prepared for what happened next. In a moment, she pulled down my rubber pants and ran away. Not knowing better, I just kept plodding down the road with my pants around my ankles.

Leaves rustled in the breeze and dogs barked as I walked, my rubber pants swishing on the ground with each step. Oblivious that anything was wrong, I simply waddled down the middle of the street, looking about, continuing to discover the world.

When nearly a block from my attacker, a second red-haired girl, older than the first but related to her I later learned, ran up to me and pulled my pants back up. More confused than alarmed, I continued on my way. In time, a familiar looking white house appeared. Home. But from that day on I have been cautious in unfamiliar places and more than a little leery of red-haired girls.

Memories are created by events that have meaning to our lives. The more significant the event, the clearer the memory. One memory that stands out very clearly is of my father reading stories to me. This was meaningful, not only because this period of my life was so brief, but because the sharing of anything, even time, was rare in my family.

My parents had purchased a set of books from a door-to-door salesman. Fifteen large red books with gold trim. I recall the night the salesman sat with my parents in the living room, telling them how "All the world's knowledge and history could be found in these books." As a "bonus," he offered to add a set of storybooks, and what a bonus they turned out to be.

The salesman made these books sound miraculous, and so they were. Miraculous because, after they arrived, and for a few brief months, I sat close beside my father on the sofa each evening, as with one or another of the big books on his lap, he read to me; *Uncle Remus*, *The Deerslayer*, *The Brothers Grimm*, and many others. And dimly I recall looking up at him, young and lean then, as he shared some of his precious time with me.

The events surrounding my childhood, taking my place as the fourth of four children, forever the "baby" of the family, are only memories now. But they are good memories. America was recovering from World War II and was growing. Families took care of their elders and people left their doors unlocked. We had coaster wagons, outhouses, back fences, and neighbors who shared party lines and more, much more. It was a time of innocence and friendships that were supposed to last forever.

Many young people today take so much for granted, as though color televisions, computers, cellphones, and palm-pilots have always existed, as if anyone who lived before these things must be from the Dark Ages. But, country schools and rural electrification, iceboxes and drive-in theaters weren't that far back in time. And modern conveniences, though new, aren't necessarily a step forward, for they often detract from those most important things, the simple things, time together and sharing.

Chapter 4
The Boies Addition

O*ur small neighborhood outside the city provided a unique environment for a boy to grow up in during the 1950's. Suburban living was not coveted then as it is today, for then it was the city dwellers who had access to services, shopping and jobs. Nearly all of the better jobs were both available and handy to those who lived in the city.*

Even farmers were better off than we were for they could grow much of their own food, and agriculture was a major industry. But those living in the Boies Addition were working-class people; people who perhaps could not afford to live in the city. But, while we didn't have a lot, we didn't miss what we didn't know about.

Before being annexed into the city, the Boies Addition was a simple community, a cluster of homes on the edge of town. Bounded on the south by the city yet surrounded by farmland and fields, it was the perfect place for a young boy who knew no bounds to grow up.

Ours was a neighborhood of unlocked doors, where friends dropped by unannounced, where boys visited their friends and, instead of knocking, stood outside and called out the name of the boy they sought.

Families were close-knit, working together on school projects, the 4-H float, or taking food to anyone who was ill. So close were we, in fact, that kids frequently called the parents of their friends, "Ma" and "Pa." There was "Ma Kinservik," "Ma DeGarmo," "Ma Keeter," "Ma

Phillips," and so on. Our friends and their families were extensions of our own.

We didn't live in fancy houses, just adequate homes, utilitarian, each one different in design and varying even more in neatness. Some were well trimmed and surrounded by flowers, others unkempt and cluttered. "Hey! Don't you be throwin' that away now. You don't know. It might be needed sometime. Then whatcha gonna do?" And while our yard didn't have trash lying about, still it was not the neatest. But then, how could it be with four active children?

A gnarled old boxelder tree stood in our front yard to which I had nailed boards to facilitate climbing. There, high in its branches, I could see fields of corn and peas and hay, and the city airport with its grass landing strip. Beyond that stretched still more farmland. I could even see Lake Koshkonong, over ten miles away.

Down the Black Bridge Road, west of my home, was the city dump, an archery range, and the Janesville Sand and Gravel Company's quarry, all favorite places to play.

Scattered throughout our neighborhood, massive elm trees formed great and graceful arches. In the summer we enjoyed their beauty and cooling shade, as did the abundant bird life, until Dutch elm disease and DDT ended the lives of both.

Highway 26 formed the eastern edge of our neighborhood where Gladys McLaughlin operated a small store from her home. There, she offered essentials, bread and milk and, of course, candy for her "kidlets," the neighborhood children. The younger kids often bought penny candy or frozen treats at Gladys' while waiting for friends. Second only to the neighborhood well, Gladys' was a favorite meeting place.

Gladys knew every boy and girl in our neighborhood and treated each one as special. She often hired one or more of us to mow her lawn or rake leaves, paying us with treats. And though we vied for the privilege, she refused to play favorites, giving each child a turn and, at the same time, a lesson in hard work and doing a thorough job. A strong work ethic prevailed in our community.

Slick's tavern stood across the street from the grocery. A small white building, it had a bar with a foot rail, a dozen or so stools, six or seven tables, and the lingering smell of many years of tobacco smoke and spilled beer.

A "pub" it was, in every sense, a place for the neighborhood men to gather after work. In my family, we jokingly referred to it as Dad's "office" because if he wasn't at work or home, we knew we could find him there.

It wasn't unusual for children to be there either. That's where I learned to play cards, watching my father play euchre and cribbage. Before long I was invited to play too, although I was just a boy.

"Hey Donnie. Smittie's not here yet. Why don't you sit in for him 'til he comes." That was a great feeling, being part of the grownup's circle. But at a dollar a game and quarter a bump, I couldn't afford it. No matter. "I'll spot you the money if we lose."

Chet's Sundry Shop was across from Slick's on Milton Avenue. Two large windows were framed by its front, and tables and booths lined the walls. Chet's was a typical soda shop of the era, a gathering place for teen's just as Slick's was for the men of the neighborhood.

While everyone got their drinking water from the community well, rainwater was used for washing clothes and bathing. And sewage disposal? Unheard of.

Trash pickup was unknown too. We burned what was burnable. This was long before there was any thought about pollution. When trash piled up, Dad simply loaded it into a trailer and hauled it to the dump. "You wanna ride along?" he would ask me. "You bet," I always replied. That was one of my favorite places for adventure.

One corner of our basement was devoted to storing the dusty, black coal that heated our home in the winter. When required, a truck from Janesville Ice and Coal Company delivered it, pouring the coal down a chute into our basement with a rumble and crash that shook the house. Mom disliked the black dust that was raised, but, except for the slightly sweet odor, I scarcely noticed.

The coal fueled the massive furnace that loomed in the center of our basement. During cold weather, it stood like a fat, silvery monster with great, uplifted arms, slits in the furnace door like angry eyes revealed red flames from the burning coal.

The first one up in the morning had to shake the clinkers down to rid the firebox of ashes, then stoked the furnace with a shovel or two of coal. Dad was usually the one to do this. This task was repeated occasionally throughout the day. Then, at least once each week, someone had the dirty job of shoveling the accumulated ashes from the bottom of the furnace. Being the youngest, I usually escaped this chore.

People take refrigeration for granted today, but it wasn't so long ago that many families couldn't afford a refrigerator. Before we had one, we kept perishables in an uninsulated entryway in the winter. Other times of year we kept food cold in an "ice box," an insulated chest lined with tin or galvanized metal.

The coalman in the winter became the iceman other times of the year, delivering large blocks of ice, chipping them to fit, hoisting them over his shoulder to place in the icebox. He knew how much to bring by a card placed in the window. Since our home was never locked, he delivered ice whether we were home or not. People were trusted then, much more than they are today.

Like many others, Mom canned much of what she grew in her small garden. She canned meats like chicken and venison too, storing them on shelves in the basement. I thought the meat looked terrible, an awful brown or yellow with a layer of fat floating on top, but it was very tender.

Monday was laundry day; evident by the clothes that hung on the lines throughout our neighborhood. My mother used an old ringer washer, transferring clothes from the wash tub to a rinse tub by hand, running them through a pair of rollers each time.

Even in the winter clothes were hung outside. Mom brought them in from the line frozen stiff and stood them in a corner to thaw before she could iron and put them away.

And few people had television early in the 1950's. We knew who did by the antennae atop their homes. The first television I ever saw was Schultzie's, a nine-inch black-and-white screen.

Telephones are so common today, many families having a phone for each member. But we had a single telephone on a telephone line shared with others. Known as "party lines," two to four homes were on the same line, with incoming calls to one number distinguishable from another by its unique ring. It was not uncommon to pick up the telephone and find someone else on the line. Nor was it uncommon to listen in on another's conversation.

So, while we didn't have the conveniences city people had, we had something they didn't. Real community.

Chapter 5
Family Life

T*he strength of a nation can be measured by the bonds that hold its people together. One essential and primary bond is "family." In our neighborhood, family relationships extended beyond blood kinship, merging with that of our friends. What we failed to learn at home, we learned through them.*

The word "love" was never used in our family except in the context of a story or talk about a favorite food. I'm not saying we didn't feel loved, only that its expression was rare. One vivid memory I have of this expression is of my mother sitting on the arm of my father's chair, wrapping her arms around him and giving him a hug. And the only reason I remember it is because it was so unusual.

My parents worked, Dad as a roofer, Mom a waitress. My grandma was a waitress too, at Elmer's Tower, a small sandwich shop downtown. Born today, I might have been called a "latchkey kid," had we any latches. Few of our neighbors locked their doors either.

My oldest brother, Ken had joined the Marines and left for Korea before finishing high school. Big sister Karen was usually with her girlfriends, and Chuck, seven years older than me, was on another planet as far as I was concerned. Not that I didn't see him, we shared a bedroom. But, like Ken, Chuck's friends were older than I, so we did very little together.

Grandma had lived with us since I was born. And for a while, an uncle and cousin lived with us too, crowding nine people into our small home.

Dad had only one sister, but Mom came from a large family, most of which moved to Janesville from northern Wisconsin. So, on her side I had several aunts, uncles and cousins to pattern after.

They were a fun loving and boisterous group who got together nearly every weekend to eat, play penny-ante poker and share a few beers. But one day while so gathered, we all learned a valuable lesson on how quickly a "penny-ante" card game can get out of hand. The dealer said, "Ante up. We're playing "In Between.""

Now "In Between" is a simple card game where each player antes a given amount, usually two cents, never more than a nickel. Two cards are dealt to one player, face up, and that player might bet any amount from a penny to the "pot" on whether a third card would fit between the first two in numerical order. If the player won, they took from the pot what was bet. If they lost, they put that amount in.

The pot began with fifty cents, and someone bet the pot... and lost. Having to match those fifty cents, the pot was now a dollar, already a large amount for our family. Then someone else tried and lost, again doubling the pot. again

For a while, players bet smaller amounts, winning some, losing most, and the pot grew. Occasionally someone received two very good cards, perhaps a two and King, and bet a larger amount. Again, they lost.

In this way, the pot continued to grow until it was nearly twenty dollars. By this time, everyone was anxious, especially Dad. He knew someone might get hurt or angry in a situation like this, but he was unsure how to prevent it. Finally, someone "bet the pot" again – and again they lost.

Now the pot stood at forty dollars, a long way from "penny ante." Everyone was eyeing it with anticipation about winning and worrying about losing. Several players bet a dollar or two, winning some, losing some, and the cards continued around the table. Finally, it was Dad's turn. He drew an ace and a king.

Since the ace could be either high or low, he elected that it be low saying, "Alright, it's time we end this game now before someone gets hurt, and we're not playing this game again."

So, Dad "bet the pot," and his third card fell. Another king! He lost. He too had to match the pot, now eighty dollars, more than a week's pay.

Angrily, he put his money on the table, fuming about the dangers of such a game. Then Grandma, who sat next to Dad, was dealt her cards, a deuce and a king.

"Oh my!" she said, and without a moment's hesitation shouted, "I bet the pot." Her third card fell. An eight. She won. A lesson learned and a game never played in our home again.

My parents taught me many lessons. Sometimes these lessons were in the form of well-earned discipline. I learned the taste of soap early on, but spanking was the general rule. Mom's spankings were never the punishment she meant them to be though, and after I began laughing at her for spanking me, she gave up and resorted to threats. "Just you wait until your father comes home, then you're really gonna get it."

Dad rarely spanked me, though he once chastened me with something far more affective. While still a preteen, I had been caught vandalizing an old shack in the woods, an abandoned girl's camp beside the Rock River known as Camp Cheerio. The punishment meted out to me by the court was to clean the place up. Dad had to go along to supervise.

Dad was never deliberately mean to me, but while piling up the accumulated trash he looked around, shook his head and said to me, "I don't know when I'll be able to trust you again. It'll probably be years, if ever." Those words and the truth of his statement hurt worse than any beating, and I was careful never to get caught doing anything like that again.

A short man with blue eyes and red hair, Dad was lean, wiry, and extremely hardworking. Bull headed and tough as nails, he backed down to no man as I discovered one day.

A friend and neighbor of Dad's, Val Phillips, stopped by to visit one afternoon. Also a small man, Val had a quick smile and equally quick wit. He and Dad shared a couple of beers and some stories, then when suppertime neared, Val excused himself to go home.

Leaving, he crossed our yard and the front lawn of our neighbor when we heard a loud voice boom out, "Hey! Get off my grass! Damn you!"

There were no sidewalks in our neighborhood, so one had to walk across lawns or in the road. Val said, "What do you want me to do, walk in the street?"

"Yeah! That's exactly what I want you to do. Now get off my lawn!"

"Well, I'm not about to," Val said. With that, the neighbor and a second man rushed towards Val. Striding up to him, the man yelled and called him foul names, then when within reach of Val, struck him squarely in the face.

Seeing this, Dad rushed out to Val's aid. The bigger man tried to push Dad aside and within moments, the four were throwing fists. Dad got hold of the bigger man, threw him to the ground, and in another minute, the fight was over.

The scuffle was brief, but in the end and for many years after Dad claimed there had been no real fight. "Little more than a wrestling match," he said, but to us kids it was a "Battle Royal." We had watched in fear and dread as the two smaller men fought the larger pair. And afterward we stood in awe and with no little respect for how the two had stood their ground.

Mom was as hard working as Dad. Escaping from the depths of the Depression, both learned not to waste anything. They knew the difference between "wants" and "needs." They didn't need a new house, they needed shelter; they didn't need a new car, they needed transportation. Likewise, new clothes were not a need. Suitable clothing was. Mom made and repaired our clothes, and we wore hand-me-downs with patches.

With nothing to waste, Mom supplemented our groceries by raising a vegetable garden, canning much of it. Opening the kitchen door, I was frequently greeted by the aroma of food being canned.

An unsuspecting contributor to our larder was Libby's Canning Company. They raised vegetables in fields down the road from our home. At harvest time, truck after truck passed our home piled high, some with pea vines bound for the cannery. Occasionally, great masses of vines fell onto the road where I gathered and carried them home. Mom and Grandma delighted in this unexpected bounty and sat in our backyard shucking peas to can.

Since such finds made them so happy, I got the idea to "help" the peas fall off. Recruiting some friends, we hid in a ditch near the highway as a truck filled with pea vines stopped at the stop sign where we rushed from cover and leaped onto the rear of the truck. Pulling armloads of pea vines off, we quickly dragged them into the ditch where we divided our booty and carted it home in wagons. Because Libby's had so much, I considered myself another Robin Hood.

"Oh, my! Look at the bunch you found this time," Grandma said as I pulled my overflowing wagon into the yard. "Where did you get so many peas? I can't imagine they could lose so much and not know it."

But after bringing home a couple more loads of "found" peas, a truck stopped in from of our home and the driver got out. To the amazement of my mother and grandmother, he came back and said, "Folks. Why don't you come take as many peas as you want. I'm afraid somebody's going to get hurt pretty soon jumping on the back of my truck that way." This brought to an end my enterprise.

We were forbidden to "waste" food, yet I was a fussy eater. Many times, I was made to sit at the table until my food was gone. Thank God for pets. Pets had always been a part of our family and we often brought home stray animals, baby birds, rabbits or mice.

My parents put up with nearly everything we brought home, including a young crow Chuck found. The crow ate dog food from a bowl with Boots, our cocker spaniel, and Boots seemed to enjoy the friendship, allowing the crow to ride on her back. Dad said he had heard crows could learn to talk if their tongues were split, but we never tried it.

Near the end of summer, the crow's welcome wore out. He began pulling clothespins from the clothesline, spilling Mom's fresh laundry onto the ground. We kids thought this was funny, but Mom saw things differently.

"That does it. Chuck. Take that crow out of here. That's the umpteenth time he's knocked my clothes off the line, and I've had it with him."

So, Chuck took his pet crow to a farmer friend who said, "Why not? What's one more?"

We had other forms of entertainment besides pets and play. Dad entertained us with his amazing agility, walking on his hands throughout the house. And he played the harmonica.

At our country school, students were offered musical instruments. Chuck opted for the cornet. Loud and brassy, he practiced long and hard. His practice was hard on the rest of us as well. But when Karen chose the saxophone, I longed to hear Chuck's cornet instead. When my turn came, I was asked what I wanted to play. Without hesitation, I said the drums. I got an accordion.

I practiced for weeks while locked up in my parent's bedroom. I say "locked up" though I wasn't actually. I only felt like a prisoner as I wrestled that cumbersome instrument. But it got the best of me as I couldn't get the hang of punching the correct buttons on the left hand

and keys on the right, while squeezing the contraption at the proper rate.

Whether from my whining or that of the accordion, my folks finally agreed it was a hopeless effort and we returned the instrument. I never got the drums I wanted.

The feeling of "family" extended beyond our own home to include many of our neighbors. Ma Hoff was one of these. Wielding indisputable authority in her own home, she was the ruler of her family. She commanded respect. I later grew to believe that respect was "earned" rather than "commanded," but around her, I didn't question how she got it.

She was no tyrant though. A seemingly coarse woman, she had a pockmarked face and dull dusty-brown hair. She wore disheveled clothing, her house was unkempt, and her voice thundered when she spoke. The neighborhood knew when she was on a rampage. Having grown up in the hills of Missouri, her early life was difficult, and her education limited. This was clear by her behavior and her speech. Not that she didn't have a good vocabulary, but it was her delivery that got your attention.

"Arnold! What did I tell you about bringing beer into this house? Now get out of here with it." And out he went.

Many times, Bud and I found Arnold in the garage, "working on the car." Other neighbors may have thought his car was in a poor state of repair, judging by how much time he spent on it. But Bud and I knew what he was doing. He bought beer in quart bottles and hid it in the garage. It was our job to watch the back door for the first sign of Ma so we could warn him in time to hide his beer before he was caught.

Ma's children were sometimes torn between their loyalty to her or to their father, developing a form of honesty that was admirable, for in spite of her apparent coarseness Ma demanded loyalty, respect and above all, honesty from her children.

"Bud! What's this I hear about you and that Kelsey girl! Didn't we talk about this before?"

"Ma. Don't make me tell you about it Ma. I might have to lie to you, and I don't want to do that. I admit, I did something I shouldn't have, Ma, I did wrong. I'm sorry I did it, and I won't do it again, Ma, I promise. Just don't make me tell you what it was."

So, Bud's mother accepted his confession of wrongdoing and sent him away with a stern warning not to do it again, whatever "it" was, and Bud always said, "I won't Ma, I promise." And that was good enough for her. She accepted his word and he meant to keep it... as best he could.

It wasn't only Ma Hoff's kids who were burned by the heat of her wrath. I felt it as well and never forgot Ma's admonitions.

"Donny Allison! God's gonna get you for that!"

I heard this threat many times, and while it didn't make me correct my ways, it did make me wonder about God and Justice.

Mr. Kinservik knew about God. The father of my friend Mike, Mr. Kinservik was an Elder in his church and was a devoted Christian, evident not only at mealtime when he gave thanks, but in his life overall. He, like Ma Hoff, was unafraid to speak to the offspring of others, teaching them the lessons of life, and though I might not have thought so at the time, I was fortunate to be such a recipient.

While visiting with Mike one day, he and I went bounding up the stairway to his room. In my exuberance, I punched the wall with my fist. Much to my surprise, my fist went through the wall, leaving a gaping hole. Mike's face went pale. I was stunned. Mr. Kinservik, having heard the noise, came to investigate. What followed was a demand that I not return until my father had repaired the damage.

Some months later, I bumped into Mr. Kinservik on the street, and he asked when my father intended to repair the wall.

"What? Do you mean you never told your father what you did?" he asked in disbelief. I hung my head in shame, as well I should. Mr. Kinservik hadn't repaired the damage. Instead, he left the hole as he said he would, for my father to repair. The hole became a daily lesson for his children about responsibility, and about choosing the right kind of friends. Clearly, I was not the kind of friend he wanted his son to be with.

The wall was repaired shortly after that, while I learned an additional lesson, the likes of which I'll never forget. It was through experiences and families like these that taught boys and girls in our neighborhood their roles and responsibilities as family members, and to one another.

Chapter 6
He Ain't Heavy, He's My Brother

S ibling rivalry existed in our family as it has in every family since Cain and Abel. Although my older brother Ken and I were not the best of friends, with our vast difference in age, we simply had little in common.

My oldest brother, Ken, was born ten years before me, so by the time I began walking and talking, he was already in school and developing into the person he was to become. I suppose it was because of our age difference that we did very little together. In fact, the only thing we did, it seems, was fight. We rarely talked, never talked in fact, except in a teasing, argumentative way. Thus, our relationship was distant at best.

Ken, I felt, was Dad's pal, while I was just a kid. He and Dad hunted together, fished together, they even worked together. Because Ken was so much closer in age to Dad, it was natural for them to do things together.

Like many others of Norwegian ancestry, Ken was blue-eyed, blond, lean and strong. And by the time he turned seventeen he was fiercely independent. Unlike me, Ken was self-confidant and outgoing, having many friends, all of them well beyond my age.

His pals were the "big kids," young men actually, for Ken was just months away from quitting high school to join the Marines while I was just a boy doing boyish things. And so, I had to find my own friends, someone closer to my own age to play with.

Late one summer day, his last summer at home before going off to see the world, Ken was playing football with his buddies in a field across the street from our home. I was playing with Ronnie in front of his home nearby. Ken and his friends were playing rough-and-tumble, passing, running, tackling, all without the benefit of padding, and we admired their strength and skill.

Ronnie and I had no football, but we wished we could play as the big kids did. Using our imaginations, we pretended we were football players too, tumbling and rolling in the grass, doing somersaults as though being tackled.

On one play, I dove over an imaginary opponent toward the goal line. Somersaulting into the ditch, I landed on an unseen broken bottle that cut deeply into my back, just missing my spine. Immediately, I knew I was hurt. Not the kind of hurt that kids feel a dozen times a day but hurt in a way where I knew I needed help. And as any seven-year-old would be, I was frightened.

I leaped to my feet, blood gushing, and ran screaming for home. Ken heard my cries, saw me running, and saw the blood streaming down my back. He knew I was in trouble.

Before I was halfway home, I felt myself being lifted up and carried, face down. Ken had scooped me up and ran with me in his arms.

He called for Mom as he ran into the house. She was working in the kitchen and immediately told him to lay me on the kitchen table. I looked up and saw him covered in blood, my blood.

Mom was always quick to act when any of us kids were hurt, which was often. I guess she instinctively knew what to do, having grown up with six brothers herself. She grabbed some towels and pressed them against my back as Ken got the car ready. Then he carried me to the car, laying me face down on Mom's lap, and within minutes, we were at the hospital.

I remember the antiseptic smell of the hospital and the clink of tools in the emergency room as the doctor picked broken glass from my back. I remember feeling the tug of the thread as he stitched my back closed again. I remember the gauze patch that covered my stitches for several days afterward too. And I remember once, some years later, hearing Ken say one of his favorite songs was, *He Ain't Heavy, He's My Brother.*

Ken and I rarely talk yet today. And I don't know if he has ever thought again of the day he carried me home bleeding. But I think of it every now and then, and of him, and always when I'm reminded of that old song.

Chapter 7
Go Tell Ma She Wants You

*J*ust like Wally and "Beaver" Cleaver of television fame, my brother, Chuck and I shared a bedroom. We didn't get along quite as well as those imaginary television brothers did though. And like many youngsters, I wondered whether I had been adopted. And no wonder. Chuck told me I was. But then, he told me lots of things.

My brother Chuck was the prankster in our family. A blue-eyed blond with a crew cut, he was seven years older than I and loved to tease. With an impish grin, he might tell me almost anything and I would believe him. And, why not? He was my big brother while I was just an innocent – no – a naïve young boy, who naturally looked up to him.

Older boys don't like having a kid brother around. Chuck was no different. He often said things to me like, "Why don't you go play in the street." Or "Hey! Did you hear that?"

"Hear what," I'd say.

"I think I heard Ma calling you."

"No, she didn't."

"Yeah, she did. You better go tell Ma she wants you." So off I'd go to see what she wanted.

Chuck was noted for his sayings too, one of which was "Let's not and say we did." This had myriad uses, such as when something had to be done that he didn't want to do, or if something was worthy of bragging about had he actually done it.

As a family, we were rarely all together at one time, so I found it strange one day to look outside and see my entire family gathered. Some neighbors were there too, so I was not only curious but also apprehensive that something might be wrong.

Investigating, I joined them. Walking up to Chuck who was nearest to me in the group, I asked what was happening. He looked at me and said in all seriousness, "The world is coming to an end tomorrow." This was said in such an honest and straightforward way that I had no doubt he was telling the truth. Besides, I hadn't yet learned to lie – not like he could anyway.

I was devastated by this news. Wordlessly, I turned and walked away, my mind flooded with thought. Hopping on my sister's bike, I rode away, my eyes filled with tears. While riding, I thought to myself how unfair life was. Here I was, just a boy, about to die without having had a chance to live yet, to experience life as others had. There is no way to express the grief I felt.

Pedaling aimlessly, I felt grievously dismayed. Nothing more could possibly go wrong, I thought when, with a "plop," something hit my shoulder. I looked and saw that a bird flying overhead had – "indiscreted" on me. That's when I learned, no matter how bad things might seem they could get worse.

Chuck was very neat and meticulous. At dinner, he looked in his water glass for anything that might be floating in it. He wiped his silverware and his dinner plate on his shirt to be sure they were clean, removing all traces of anything real or imagined.

Chuck was so fussy about having things done right that, while Mom cut everyone else's hair, he cut his own. With a comb and electric trimmer, he seated himself in one chair with a mirror on another. Then he carefully trimmed the top and sides, paying particular attention to getting each side exactly the same, and the top level. This created what was called a "flattop." He cut rearward as far as he could, sometimes placing a second chair and mirror behind to aid him. But inevitably, he had to allow Mom to finish the back.

Being so fastidious, it was no surprise that he didn't like sharing a bedroom with a boy like me. Our room was large. In it were two windows, a double bed, and a large chest of drawers. We had a large open closet in which were, among other things, my toy box, an old guitar with two broken strings, and a wooden shoeshine box that Chuck had made as a 4-H project, but in which were kept marbles.

A pair of heavy curtains supported by a thick wooden dowel fronted our closet. I often used the curtains as a swing, tying the ends together and sitting on the knot. With this, I would swing, seemingly for hours, my feet and head alternately touching the ceiling.

But one day I decided to swing in another way. Chuck and I had been left home alone and he had teased me endlessly. Finally, unable to take any more of his teasing, I ran upstairs to our room screaming, "I'll fix you!" In my toy box, I kept a lariat, given to me by my grandma's boyfriend, Nick. It was made of half-inch rope and was very strong.

While standing on Chuck's shoeshine box, I put the rope over the curtain rod, then placed the loop around my neck. Holding firmly to the end of the rope, I was just about to jump off the box when Chuck came upstairs to investigate.

He saw me standing on the box with the rope around my neck and said, "What do you think you are doing?" Angrily, I told him I was going to hang myself. He simply looked at me and said, "If you do, I'll tell Ma." Then he turned and went back downstairs.

That scared me. I thought, "If Ma found out I'd hung myself, she'd kill me." So, I took the rope off, put it away, and went outside to play.

Because we shared a bedroom with only one bed, Chuck had many other opportunities to take advantage of me. One of his favorites was, "You scratch my back, I'll scratch yours." I always enjoyed having my back scratched, so I readily agreed.

"OK. You go first," he said. So, I scratched his back until I tired of it and thought it was my turn. But Chuck said, "Just another minute." So, I scratched his back for another minute. Then, when it was finally my turn, he pretended to be asleep.

When I finally got wise to his trickery, Chuck invented variations, suggesting we count the freckles on each other's back, or write something with our finger with the other person having to guess what was written. Chuck would do anything to have his back scratched.

He and I had a couple pair of boxing gloves, made of well-worn, softly padded leather. Actually, we didn't have two pairs, but one-and-a-half. I never learned where or when the fourth glove disappeared, but we put the three gloves to good use.

In his characteristically magnanimous way, Chuck gave me the complete pair while he used the single glove himself, and our bed became our boxing ring. Armed as we were, I stood up while Chuck knelt on his knees to spar. Swinging my arms like double windmills, I tried my best to hit him, but as his reach was much longer than mine, I rarely touched him. With one arm, he held me away with his ungloved hand, and pummeled me with the other.

Again, Chuck found a variation on this sport, but one I learned to avoid after a single occasion. He said, "Let's see who can hit the softest."

Well, I thought, what's the harm in hitting soft? So, I agreed. "You go first," he said, and I did, touching him so gently, he hardly knew I hit him. Then he slugged me, knocking me off my feet while loudly declaring me to be the winner.

Chuck and I shared a fishing adventure once, walking to Goose Island, now called Traxler Park. We used stale bread for bait, soaking it with water and kneading it into a dense paste. Covering our hooks with a ball of this bait, we cast into the lagoon and settled back to wait for the tug of a fish. Carp were great fun to catch, whether big or small.

Late one afternoon we headed home, walking up Saint Mary's hill, passing some boys who were playing in front of their house. One jeered at us for being in "their" neighborhood, as the others sneered. The first picked up a garden hose and sprayed us with water, thoroughly soaking us. Chuck simply continued walking, not wanting to fight. But I was angry and lashed out with my fishing rod, striking the boy.

My hook buried itself in his clothes and maybe into his skin. With a surprised look on his face, the boy dropped the hose. I'm sure he didn't know what to think, whether I might tug and sink the hook deeper or swat him again. I was ready to do either if need be. The boy quickly removed the hook and dropped it.

Retrieving my hook, we continued on our way, followed by the boy's threats against passing through his neighborhood again. Chuck chided me for striking out as I had, saying, "You shouldn't have done that. You could get us in trouble." But I felt I was only defending myself, and I continued to look behind us until the boys were out of sight.

Chuck and I did have some good times together, like the summer night we slept out under the stars. We had a pair of Army surplus sleeping bags, given to us by my uncle Orval. They were the itchy kind, stiff heavy wool that smelled of mothballs. The bags were shaped like mummies and fit like cocoons. To get into them, one slipped his legs into the small hole at the top and pulled it on like a large stocking.

A drawstring around the hole closed the bag leaving only the face exposed.

Chuck and I lay on the ground between our house and our neighbor's, staring into the night sky, watching stars and counting meteors late into the night. This was one of the few times we wondered together and talked seriously about life. Stars in the evening sky will do that.

But Chuck resumed his prankster ways the next night as I lay in bed reading a comic book. The bedroom window was open beside me, warm summer air blowing the curtains gently while a neighbor's dog howled in the distance. Suddenly, a hand came through the window just inches away from my face. Screaming, I threw my comic book into the air and struggled to run for my life. Then I heard laughter outside. Chuck and his friend Bill were outside my window on the kitchen roof. They laughed so hard they nearly fell off.

A few days later I had an opportunity to get even with Chuck. He was dating a girl and came home late. At breakfast, Mom asked what time he got in, to which he replied, "Oh, I don't know, not too late though."

This gave me an idea. That night Chuck was going out again, so I fixed a length of cord to the dresser and strung it across the doorway, tying the other end to the old guitar in our closet. On top of the guitar, I placed shoes, toys, and our box of marbles. Then I went to bed to await the results.

Later that night, when Chuck came home, quite naturally he tripped over the cord. The guitar fell with a tremendous crash. My toys clattered and marbles rattled, and my dad's voice boomed from downstairs, "What the hell was that?"

The next few seconds seemed like an eternity. The only sound was that of marbles rolling across the wood floor.

Mom came hurrying up the stairs, making rather ominous sounds herself, and in the ensuing confusion I never got a chance to ask her what time it was.

Chapter 8
Never Hit Girls

My sister Karen was all right, I guess, for a girl. Unfortunately, it took me twenty years to realize it. Until then, she was nothing but trouble for me. But then, I suppose I got as much as I gave.

My sister was a skinny, knobby-kneed, freckle-faced girl with red hair, blue eyes and an impish smile. Three years older than I, Karen was my only sister and a source of great aggravation. Unlike me, she had her own bedroom, which was just one of the aggravating things about her. She also had a bicycle. That, to a young boy with places to go, was humiliating.

I rode her bike on occasion, especially those occasions when she wasn't around to stop me. For me, having anything to ride was enough. And at my age, I felt no disgrace riding a girl's bike. That stigma wasn't felt until junior high school. By then I would walk miles before being caught on a girl's bike.

When I was still a toddler, we had no running water in our home and had to conserve what little there was. Our Saturday night baths were almost a ritual experience, with several people having to share the same few inches of water in the bathtub.

Since I was so young, Mom made Karen and I bathe together. Karen, perhaps taking her cue for teasing from her older brothers, once told me, "If you're not good, the devil's gonna cut that off." I, not yet old enough to ask if she was speaking from experience, simply thought she was more knowledgeable than I was because she was older.

One day while expressing my curiosity, as I often did, I climbed onto the kitchen counter to investigate a new gadget Mom had recently bought. It was a vegetable slicer with a razor-sharp blade. I know it was razor sharp because as I ran my finger across its edge, Karen came into the room and yelled at me to get down.

Startled, I jumped, cutting my finger badly. Hearing my cries, Mom came running. She saw me bleeding profusely, and as she bound my wound, Karen poured ashes into it by telling Mom how she caught me climbing on the counter where I wasn't supposed to be.

I never intended to cause my sister any pain, though I once did inadvertently. My brothers often came to the dinner table, and to be smart, rather than pulling a chair out to sit down, they simply swung a leg over the back, like a cowboy mounting a horse. I thought this was pretty keen, and wished I were as grown up as they were so I could do it too.

Well, one afternoon my sister sat on the couch beside our mother as Mom was teaching her how to crochet. I stood before them watching, when suddenly I got one of those ideas that seem to come to small boys from out of the blue. Like my brothers swinging their legs over the chairs at dinnertime, I wanted to see if I could swing my leg over my sister's head. I neared Mom and Karen until I judged I was at just the right distance, then in one swift, smooth motion, I kicked Karen squarely in the nose.

My, but she cried. Blood trickled from her nose while tears poured from her eyes, and Mom, with a sigh of exasperation, calmly asked, what in the world I did that for. Then she listened as I, as startled by the results as anyone, unsuccessfully tried to explain.

A short time later, Dad instructed me that boys were never to hit girls. This didn't seem fair to me, especially since I thought Karen might benefit from an occasional poke.

Consider this instance. A sidewalk abutted our concrete garage. This combination of hard surfaces was perfect for a boy to throw a ball against, caroming off the garage and returning in a high loop. Or, hitting the garage first, the ball might bounce off the sidewalk and back to me in a line drive.

I became so adept that I could hit specific spots, like the juncture of the sidewalk and the garage, which produced a popup, or for variation, the edge of the sidewalk, resulting in a ground ball.

One day, I was minding my own business as usual, just bouncing a golf ball against the garage and catching it in my baseball mitt. Karen had hung some clothing on the clothesline near where I was playing. This didn't bother me. I still had plenty of room to play catch by myself. But evidently it wasn't enough room for her, for she promptly came out of the house and told me to play somewhere else.

"No," I said.

"Get away from my clothes before you get them dirty."

"I ain't hurting anything of yours. Besides, I was here first."

That seemed like sound enough reasoning to me, and I believed she felt it was too, because she went back in the house. But, not for long. In less than a minute she was back, and she was carrying a broom.

"Get away from my clothes before I hit you with this," she said.

"No! I haven't touched your dumb clothes, and I ain't moving."

"You'll move all right," she said, and she raised the broom to strike me.

As the broom handle came down, I blocked it with one arm and grabbed it, yanking it away from her. At that moment, Dad came out of the house, having heard the commotion. There I stood with the broom in my hands.

"Don! What do you think you're doing?" he shouted.

"She tried to..."

"Don't you know any better?"

"I was..."

"What did I just tell you? Don't you EVER hit a girl!" he bellowed, as he stormed up to me.

"But she hit me!"

"I don't care. I don't ever want to catch you hitting a girl."

"Why not?" I asked, thinking girls deserved as good as they gave.

"Never mind why. Just do as I say." With that, Karen grabbed the broom from me and went back into the house. Dad, after giving me a look that said he meant business, turned and followed.

I returned to my game of catch, wondering about what had just transpired and the justice – or injustice – I had witnessed. Anyway, I thought I had held my ground and considered myself the winner, for I was still playing as before.

Some weeks later I was playing baseball. As usual, we were playing on the lot where the neighborhood well was located, beside Mrs. Kelly's home. Since we had only five or six on each team, there weren't enough players to cover each base, so we played "Pitcher's-Hand-Is-Out." With that game, the batter had to reach first base before the pitcher got the ball or was called out. This was "sandlot" baseball, years before Little League, umpires, or parents took over the game.

I got a hit and ran to first base before the pitcher, Danny, got the ball. Nevertheless, he called me "out." I disagreed. Tempers flared and gloves flew, and before I knew it, Danny and I were circling each other, fists clenched, ready to settle our dispute. Circling was a favorite tactic of young boys when in a fight. Circling gave a boy time to size up his opponent and look for weaknesses in his defense. More importantly, it might buy enough time to be called home for supper before any real blows were struck.

Well, I wasn't so lucky. After a few parries and thrusts without contact, as our friends surrounded us cheering for blood, from the corner of my eye I saw Karen walking down the road. Although she was probably going to McLaughlin's grocery, I hoped she was coming to tell me it was time for supper.

With my eyes off Danny for a moment, he hit me squarely on the chin, dropping me flat on my back. Lying there dazed, I looked up, not at Danny, but at Karen. She continued walking by, though now she was shaking with laughter. That broke my spirit, and so I quit the fight, and the ballgame, and went home.

Chapter 9
Scrimshaw

T*he makeup of families has changed, as has their relationship to one another, their care and support. My grandmother lived with us while I was growing up. She was my father's mother, and I never knew life might be any other way. In those days it was common for several generations of one family to live together. Not that you don't see this today, but it is seen less than in previous eras. Today we talk of single-parent families, blended families, nuclear families, extended families, and who-knows-what-kind of families. But when I was growing up, we just had family.*

Since my parents both worked, I often visited with my grandma who lived in an apartment Dad had built for her above our garage. She had lived with us since moving from Wisconsin's north woods, separating from my grandpa. Life in the north was just too hard for her.

Entering the dark stairway leading to her apartment, I heard a rhythmic thump, thump, thump, then a pause during which there was a metallic squeak, followed again by the thumping. Grandma was making rag rugs on her loom. I flipped the switch at the foot of the stairs, lighting the single bare light bulb at the top. Her stairs were cluttered with all manner of items, a walking cane, shoes, a jar or two, a hammer, paper bags.

The rhythmic sound of the loom continued. Thump, thump, thump, squeak. Thump, thump.

At the top of the stairs, a door opened into her living room. Entering, I looked about. The thumping grew louder. The musty odor of Grandma's home, of Grandma herself, met me. Before me I saw an overstuffed chair and a heavy couch with an old print centered on the wall behind. A small lampstand held an ancient lamp topped by a faded yellow shade. There was a rocking chair and a floor lamp, and photographs on the wall, including one of her brother Leslie, the last of her eight siblings.

Leslie lived in Arizona. He was eight years older than my grandmother. I had never met him, and Grandma once told me she had seen him only a couple times since marrying Grandpa, though they exchanged letters frequently. Life had been hard, she said. Very hard.

A few knick-knacks lay about and some old figurines. Looking around the living room, I spotted a familiar item, a walrus tusk that had been carved into a cribbage board, an example of scrimshaw. On its backside was carved a polar bear swimming after a walrus, while on the front was a fish with a simple geometric design through its midsection and, of course, there were peg holes. The root-end of the tusk once had a cover, also of bone, behind which the cribbage pegs had been kept, but they had long since been lost.

A lamp stand held a shallow bowl filled with thimbles, scissors and several spools of thread. On the floor next to her rocker were balls of cloth of different colors for the rag rugs Grandma made. She cut cotton cloth from old clothing into strips an inch wide, sewing each strip together, then rolling them into balls.

When she needed cloth of a certain color, Grandma wound the cloth strips onto bobbins and passed them back and forth through the warp, pressing the cloth tightly by beating against it with the loom's heavy comb. This was the thump, thump, thump I heard day after day. When the woof was snug, she raised the heddles, crossing the warp strings to hold the woof in place. This made the squeak I heard.

Repeatedly she passed the bobbin through the warp, beating the woof tight, hour after hour.

Sunlight entered her living room through two large windows, reflecting off a glass paperweight, a souvenir from Mammoth Cave. Grandma had once visited Mammoth Cave with a man I knew only as "the balloon man." Grandma called him Nick, but that's all I ever learned of his name. Grandma didn't talk much about his personal life.

Whenever Nick visited her, he brought small gifts for me, usually balloons. One time he brought me a heavy rope, a real cowboy lariat. One end was braided into a permanent loop; the other end braided so not to unravel. This rope was my pride and joy and I quickly learned how to throw a loop over anything within reach. Every dog and cat on the block quickly grew familiar with it, running off at my approach.

Grandma and Nick traveled around the country together several times, often gone for weeks at a time. Nick was very mysterious about his work, about his comings and goings. We never knew when he might return. When I asked about him, Grandma told me I shouldn't pry, it wasn't nice.

After a couple years, Nick simply disappeared. Grandma was very sad and worried about him, not knowing what had happened. I didn't know whether they broke up or if he found someone else, but several years later Mom told me word came that he was killed in Chicago. It seems he was not just a mysterious man, but someone Grandma had known from years earlier.

The thumping continued. Across the room was Grandma's tiny bathroom. She had no running water in her apartment, though it was plumbed to drain sewage into the septic system. A garden hose ran from my parent's home into hers providing water for cooking and her toilet. But in the winter, she went without running water.

I entered her small kitchen. A tiny stove stood on my left, beside an equally small window. A metal cupboard suspended above the stove held her few dishes. Across from the stove were a table and two chairs, and near the table stood a glass-fronted curio cabinet.

Grandma sat at her loom just inside the next room, her bedroom, the most spacious room of all. Dad had added this room several years after the apartment was built, when he added a workshop for himself behind the garage. Ample windows allowed light into the room from three sides.

Absorbed with weaving a rug, Grandma was passing the bobbin back and forth through the warp, beating the woof down with the comb, all the while listening to a Milwaukee Braves baseball game on the radio. So, intent in her work was she that she had no idea I was there until I stepped closer.

"Oh! You startled me!" she said when she finally noticed, and she stopped her work to talk. Grandma's leathery, wrinkled face showed the harshness of her years. Her gray hair was rolled up in a bun, with loose wisps sticking out on both sides of her face. A dark patch of skin on her left cheek warned of the skin cancer that she was to suffer from many years later.

Behind Grandma's glasses, her eyes still sparkled, though the weight of her glasses had created folds of skin on each side of her nose, sagging like small yellow bags. She wore a long, shapeless dress. Her shoes, always black, were old-fashioned and had holes cut in them to allow room for her painful bunions. Coarse, heavy brown support hose aided the poor circulation she suffered from, which often caused her feet and legs to swell badly.

Grandma removed her hard, knobby hands from the loom's comb, placed them on her lap, and asked me to sit down. I did. Looking around the crowded room, I wondered how lonely it must be to sit here day after day.

The room was large, but the heavy loom filled much of it. Sharing this space was Grandma's double bed, a cedar chest, a large, old Philco radio and a nightstand. A door led outside to a stairway landing above

Dad's workshop behind the garage. Sheer white curtains hung in the windows, billowing in the summer breeze.

Grandma and I talked, as we often did, about her growing up in the hill country of Missouri, near Middleton. She told me about farm life, her brothers and sisters, and of the distances they had to travel to visit neighbors. She recalled how she first met Grandpa when the Allison family appeared on the horizon in a covered wagon. They settled in a valley just a couple miles away, she told me, becoming her nearest neighbors.

Grandpa was a young man then. His real mother, unable to care for him, had given him up for adoption, together with two sisters, when he was four. He never saw his sisters again. And though the Allison family took him in, they treated him very badly, she said. Then with a wide smile, she told how she and Charlie, my grandpa, eventually ran off together when she was barely sixteen, though it wasn't until she was nineteen that they finally married in Wellsville, Missouri.

As usual, Grandma had many stories to tell me. She said they moved from place to place, from Wellsville to the tiny community of Bellflower, Missouri, then to Nilwood, Illinois where Grandpa worked in a mine. When that mine closed they moved to another in Girard. After that, Grandpa got a job with Powers and Thompson Construction Company in Virden, Illinois. They eventually moved to Chicago where Grandpa worked for Anheuser-Busch until Prohibition when he opened a boarding house and café.

"Times were very hard," Grandma said, explaining how they did whatever they could to eat and keep a roof over their heads. "This was during the Prohibition times, you know, and your grandpa had to make whiskey just to get by. That's when your grandpa met and got to be friends with George Goetz."

"Goetz also went by the name George Von Ashe," she said, going on to tell me for probably the hundredth time, how the boarding house caught fire and burned, and how neighbors helped her save what they could. But when morning came, nothing was left of the building but ashes and the tall chimney with a copper condenser coil attached, waving like a flag. "That's all that was left of your grandpa's still," she said. "So that's when Goetz hired your grandpa to be caretaker of his lodge in Couderay."

She said "Your pa and grandpa moved up there in 1928. Your pa was just 14. Me and Sis came up the next summer."

She talked of the times they had in the woods of northern Wisconsin, telling of several visits by Capone and his friends. Ed O'Hare was one of them.

"They called him 'Artful Eddie,'" she said, adding, "He was a Saint Louis lawyer." Years later, I learned he was not only an attorney but also owner of the Laramie Kennel Club, a dog track known by many today as Sportsman's Park. Pressure from Capone forced O'Hare to become a partner but, "Ed didn't like Capone very much," Grandma told me.

"His boy, 'Butch' came with him a couple of times. He was a tubby little boy," she said, "but Ed thought the world of him. He grew up to become a hero," she added, explaining how O'Hare eventually testified against Capone to get Butch into the Naval Academy at Annapolis.

"Butch became a fighter pilot in the Second World War, earning the Congressional Medal of Honor, you know, for saving his ship. He got killed later though. O'Hare field in Chicago is named after him."

Grandma loved to talk about one of Capone's men who had a huge boil on his backside. He went down to the lake almost daily and out onto a long pier where he dropped his trousers to expose this sore to the sun, hoping that might cure it. Grandma laughed as she told how she and an Indian girlfriend of hers sneaked through the brush to watch him sunning himself on the pier.

She told how the men kept their hunting rifles and shotguns propped against a wall in one corner of the living room of the lodge, and a small boy who was playing near them, discharged one of the rifles.

The bullet passed through the ceiling, striking a bed upstairs, exploding a feather tick mattress and filling the room with feathers.

"Later owners of the lodge left the bullet hole," she said, "telling people it was from a gunfight."

She laughed and told me that Capone once tried to hunt deer. "Your father got some men from town to drive deer toward him. But it was cold, and Capone couldn't stand still. He waved his arms about trying to keep warm. You ask your father how his waving scared the deer away and he never got a shot."

With endless tales to tell, she told of driving to Hayward with some of Capone's men to shop. They bought her a fur coat. "They were the nicest men," she said.

"And later, when they were preparing to leave the lodge and return to Chicago, Capone gave your grandpa and your father each a gun." I was familiar with the guns she was talking about. Both Winchesters, one was a .22 and the other a shotgun.

Then she told how he had presented her with a cribbage board carved from a walrus tusk. With pride, she pointed to it in the other room, saying, "Bring it here to me."

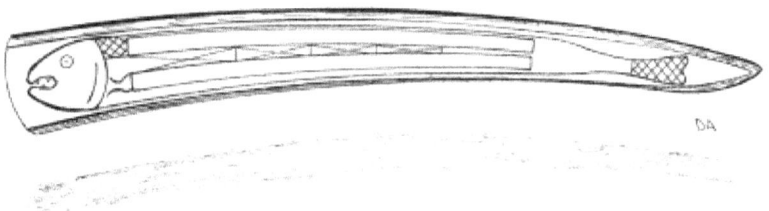

When I retrieved the tusk and returned, she told me I should have something to remind me of those days too, and to remind me of the times we sat and talked.

"I want you to have it," she said. "An Eskimo made it. It's what they call 'scrimshaw.' Take it and tell your children about your old grandma and how hard her life was."

I held the cribbage board in my hands, looking at the engravings, wondering who made it and how it ever came to be in the hands of such a man as Al Capone.

Many times, since then I have looked at that old cribbage board and thought of Grandma and how her path crossed that of the men she talked about. And when I look at it today, I think about the doors that open and paths that cross in one's life, and I wonder what is yet to come.

Chapter 10
Imagination

*K*ids have no imagination today. They don't need one, not when they have toys with moving parts and realistic sounds, books that talk, and interactive computer games. What imagination does that take?

We connected tin cans with a piece of string that, when pulled tight, allowed one person's voice to travel the length of the string to the ear of another person holding a second can. We played in cardboard boxes, pretending to drive cars or trucks. We imagined we could fly. There was no limit to what we could do with our imaginations. It's a wonder to me that any children know how to "pretend" today.

I was born with an inquiring mind, a scientific mind I like to believe. I have always asked the how and why of things. I still do. Rarely have the answer come, but the questions have always been there.

Early in my days of discovery I wondered, "If I could lift myself using a bar overhead, couldn't I lift myself with a bar beneath me just as well?" I saw no difference but for the position of the bar.

Believing I was on my way to joining the ranks of Newton, Einstein and Galileo, I wondered why no one else had ever thought of this simple experiment before. Taking a broom, I placed it under my backside. Then, lifting as hard as I dared, being careful to pull just hard enough to hold myself up but not so hard that I would bump my head on the ceiling, I quickly raised my feet. Expecting to be suspended in midair, I was amazed when I crashed to the floor, pinning my fingers painfully beneath the broom handle, ending my first experiment in free flight.

"BANG! GOTCHA!"

"Ow! Oh! But...But...Before I die...Bang! Gotcha back."

That was how we to played cowboys. Fairly. No one got the upper hand on another. Each one got shot. Each one died. Sometimes four or five cowboys could be seen staggering around at the same time, clutching his chest, dying but not yet dead, waiting to shoot the one who shot him. Then, as the last one was shot, we all fell dead together in a pile.

Our playing didn't start this way. It evolved. When Ron and Mike and other friends of mine first started playing together, we robbed each other without regard, attacked from ambush, or drew and shot one another after someone got caught cheating at cards. A boy would draw and fire his cap gun and his victim would reel and fall to the ground in the throes of death.

Most often, the boy with the most realistic guns won the gunfights.

"That ain't fair!" I cried, after being killed for the umpteenth time. It seemed I was always being killed while Ronnie had yet to bite the dust.

"But you missed me," he said.

"Did not!"

"Did too! Besides, I didn't even see you draw your gun."

Well, that was because I had to use my finger for a gun and pretend to shoot while Ronnie had a set of genuine, silver-coated plastic, Roy Rogers cap guns complete with extra rolls of caps. All I had was a finger and my imagination. Ronnie and the other kids refused to recognize my imagination as a valid weapon. They said they couldn't tell if I was pulling a gun or just pointing at them.

This led to gunfights where we shot each other a kazillion times without reloading or falling down dead, and soon we tired of saying,

"Bang! Gotcha."

"I got you too."

"Bang! Bang! Gotcha again and again."

"No you didn't. You missed!"

"Fall down."

"No! I'm not falling down. You didn't even come close. You fall down!"

"No! I'm not falling down until you fall down."

Gunfights, where no one falls to the ground dead, were no fun at all. Eventually we found it necessary to create a set of rules, the most significant rule being that everyone had to fall down and die.

Another rule we finally agreed on was that I had to use something for a gun because at every shootout we had, I could draw and shoot my finger faster than they could draw their toy guns. I never dropped my finger on the ground nor got it caught in a holster. So, I used a stick until I could carve a gun from a piece of board. That was fair. That was justice in the old Midwest.

AS A NATURAL EXTENSION of our game of Cowboys and Indians, we pretended to have saloons where we gambled. To be fair, each started with an equal amount of Monopoly® money. But once the cards were dealt, all fairness went out the window. From then on, we tried to hold cards or hide them up a sleeve, deal from the bottom, or do anything and everything to cheat, just like in the movies.

And while our pretending was only play, it taught us some great lessons, like don't gamble for real with the boy who won when we couldn't catch him cheating.

WE DIDN'T NEED FANCY toys to have a good time. We had fun simply walking in the fields that surrounded our neighborhood. In the spring we might find arrowheads or throw clods of dirt at targets. When a dirt clod struck the ground it sent up a cloud of dust like the smoke from an explosion, transforming the dirt clod into a hand grenade.

With little more than our imagination, boxes became cars and boats and airplanes, or hideouts and jails for playing cops-and-robbers. If we wanted to be musicians, they were drums. Sticks became rifles, spears, canes, telescopes or tools.

With a few pieces of string and a metal washer for a weight, a hanky or preferably, sister's scarf, became a parachute. Tying the string to each corner of the scarf and attaching the weight completed it. By rolling the scarf up and winding the string around it, one threw his "parachute" high into the air and watched the string unwind and the "chute" float gently to the ground.

No child today has better toys than what we had. And with our imaginations, our fun was inexhaustible.

Chapter 11
Winter Play

Today one hears of acid rain, El Nino, or changing weather patterns. Skeptics don't believe these changes are occurring, but winters really were different when I was a boy, and so was play.

We looked forward to winter and the many special things we could do at that time of year. One of those things was having snowball fights. Wars they were, for they sometimes lasted for days, as long as the weather was right for packing snow. Choosing teams, the entire neighborhood became our battleground with only one rule, no ice-balls.

Each side built a snow fort and stockpiled it with great masses of snowballs in preparation for battle. When our forts were within throwing distance, we lobbed snowballs like mortar shells, high into the air to rain down on our opponents. But sometimes our forts were far apart necessitating the use of coaster wagons or sleds to haul our arsenal of snowballs. When we felt we had a sufficient number of snowballs to overwhelm our "enemy" we attacked.

In a single mighty charge, one side attacked the other, snowballs flying furiously. In frenzied close-quarter fighting, kids screamed and ran back and forth, charging and counter-charging, throwing and ducking and throwing again. This kept up until our "ammunition" was exhausted, or we were. Then we regrouped to repeat our effort. Any military general would have been proud to command an army as eager for battle as we were.

There were no winners or losers, just kids having fun. By afternoon we were wet, happy and laughing together, rebuilding our forts and restocking our piles of snowballs, preparing to do battle again the next day.

Melting snow occasionally formed pools of water that re-froze in a plowed field across the road from my home. Perfect for skating, sometimes a pool formed in Mr. Schoenrock's yard, two houses away. Oftentimes someone's parents or siblings drove us to the skating rink at Goose Island, today's Traxler Park. There, a warming house with a large fireplace provided warmth and park benches to sit on. The air in the warming house was filled with the aroma of burning wood and steamy wet wool.

Skating at Goose Island was a popular pastime for people of all ages. High-school boys played hockey on the far end of the rink, the clash and crash of their sticks and scrape of their skates was heard across the ice. Eventually the city built a hockey rink on land, separating the hockey players from other skaters so people could skate in peace.

The ice-skating rink was a popular place for boys and girls to meet. Many couples would skate in tandem, arm in arm, gracefully circling the rink to music played over loud speakers. Other skaters practiced figures. But for the kids from my neighborhood, there was nothing like crack-the-whip.

For crack-the-whip, we joined arms or held hands, and skated together in a line until the lead person in line turned sharply. That caused each person farther from that end to skate faster to keep up. The trick was for those on the far end to hold on if they could, because just like a whip, centrifugal force caused them to fairly fly. Many times, one or several near the end couldn't hold on and fell in a laughing heap or flew careening into a snowbank.

I received a pair of figure skates for Christmas when I was eleven. They fit me well that winter, but by the next year I had grown. They were too small for me then, cutting off the circulation to my toes.

Unable to afford another pair of skates, I had to make do. Consequently, I had to go to the warming house regularly to loosen my skates and warm my cold feet.

Sometimes I stayed outdoors too long and got very old. One day I froze my fingers and toes. Entering the house after playing, I cried from the pain. Grandma told me, "Go get me some snow, Donny. I'll rub your hands with it. That'll fix it." This was her time-tested method for preventing frostbite. After rubbing my frozen appendages with snow, she made me soak them in cold water. Today we might use the water, but not the snow. Grandma had her own ways.

Many people claim that the snow was deeper and winters colder when they were young. And though it doesn't make sense, I have to admit it has been many years since I've seen snow like that of the '50's. Snowplows piled drifts so high we could stand on them and touch the telephone wires that ran parallel to the Black Bridge Road.

We made caves in these drifts, crawling on our bellies, burrowing and enlarging a space deep inside. I was always amazed by how warm and snug we felt there with cold, blue sunlight filtering through the snow, providing just enough soft light to see by. All sounds were muted but that of our breathing. We were in a crystalline world of our own making.

With no hills near my home to ski or slide on, I resorted to making my own "hill" by shoveling snow into a pile. It took all day to pile it high enough, but when it was ready, I climbed my hill, strapped my brother Chuck's skis to my overshoes and skied thirty or forty feet, far enough for a small boy with a big imagination.

As we grew older, Mike and Schultzie, Danny and I, and some of the other kids in my neighborhood, took our sleds and toboggans down the Black Bridge Road to the sandpit where we could glide great distances. Dodging trees and brush, we glided across frozen ponds, the same ponds we swam and fished in only a few short months earlier.

Sometimes we slid downhill on a sheet of cardboard. But usually, we used my toboggan to make the long, winding run to the bottom. When the snow was deep and loose, we dared each other to ride downhill while standing up on the toboggan. Then with each run the snow packed tighter and we went faster and farther until finally the snow was packed tightly enough for us to race down on our sleds.

Sleds worked well on ice and hard-packed snow, but when the snow was fresh and deep, the toboggan was king. If it had any fault at all it was steering. If we went too fast or had to turn sharply, we were in trouble, crashing headlong into trees. But thanks to our youth and heavy clothing, we experienced few injuries.

My brother Chuck wasn't so fortunate though. One day, while playing in my room, I heard a commotion downstairs. Mom's excited voice told me something was amiss, so I went down to investigate. There I saw two neighbor boys, Dave and Bill, carrying Chuck into the house. They had been skiing together at the sandpit when Chuck took a fall, badly spraining an ankle. Unable to walk, Chuck's friends carried him home.

Winter was an exciting time for us, not just for the fun times we had, but for the wonder and anticipation of the holidays that were just around the corner.

Chapter 12
Christmas

*H**olidays have changed. In the postwar years, holidays revolved around people, around friends and family. There was less emphasis on the commercial aspect of holidays and more on the personal, on the meaning behind the holiday. Times have changed, and in that change, I think we've lost something.*

Not only did we always have snow, but other things were different about winters in the fifties; Christmas for one thing. Businesses closed by 9:00 P.M. and were never open on Sunday. And, unlike today, businesses didn't begin to decorate for Christmas until after Thanksgiving.

A few weeks before Christmas, my mother gave me a few dollars to buy presents with. This was my introduction to wise shopping and making my money stretch. I bought practical things, ties, hankies or a billfold for Dad, hankies or a scarf for Mom, or maybe perfume from Woolworth's. But the presents I was concerned about were my own.

I hoped to get things like my friends had; a matching pair of real metal cowboy revolvers complete with leather holsters like Ronnie's. The only toy gun I had was made of plastic. And I had always wanted a B-B gun like Schultzie's, a high-powered straight-shooting Daisy.

Two brothers, Wayne and Bob, owned a realistic toy earthmover with wheels and pulleys and levers that actually worked, and a nice flat-bed truck to haul it on. Toys like that I could only dream about.

Our Christmas decorations were stored in the attic, but the attic-way was small, too small for any but me to enter easily. Therefore, it was my job to climb up and hand the boxes of decorations down to the others. Soon the tree was festooned with lights and tinsel and glass balls, items handed down over the years. We strung popcorn on sewing thread for garland, and carefully placed bubble lights where each one could be seen. A shining, silver and gold star topped our tree.

On Christmas Eve, Mom plugged the candles in that had been placed in each window. This she said was to show Santa where we lived. Each of us kids hung our stocking on the staircase where they would be within easy reach come morning. Then, it was off to bed.

I had a hard time sleeping. My folks seemed to stay up way too late doing things. I thought, "Don't they know it's Christmas?" It was hard enough to get to sleep without them rustling about. I lay in bed, anxiously wondering what gifts I would find in the morning. Usually, I received things like new pajamas or pants, shirts or underwear. But once there was a pair of marionettes, Peter Pan and Captain Hook. And the previous year, Chuck got a Lionel train set. Still wondering what might greet me in the morning, I fell asleep.

I awoke before daylight and tried to get Chuck and Karen up. They didn't want to get out of bed yet, perhaps already knowing something I didn't. Instead, they suggested I sneak down to get our stockings.

I found it hard to sneak quietly. Our bare wood floor creaked with every step. I managed to reach the stockings and, in the dim pre-dawn light, tried to see what was piled around the tree.

"Don," Mom's voice threatened. "Get back to bed!" How she knew it was me, I never knew, but I managed to get our stockings before retreating.

Taking the stockings to Chuck and Karen, we found them filled with small gifts, fruits and candies. They were but a prelude to what was to follow. Soon I attempted to sneak downstairs again. This time Mom didn't stop me, and my excitement got everyone out of bed.

The tree was surrounded with presents piled high, some leaning against the walls. Cards and cookies hung from the branches on the tree. There I spotted an earth mover and flatbed truck. Though not as nice as Wayne and Bob's, they were my very own.

Other Christmases I received a steam-powered engine, a chemistry set, and games of various kinds. Chuck got a football game with a metal playing field that vibrated to make each of the men move. He and I had hours of fun with that. And just a year earlier there was the toboggan, a gift to all of us. But one of the finest gifts we ever received was a wooden ark my dad made for us, complete with pairs of wooden animals he had carved and hand painted. I still have and treasure some of these.

The smell of food filled our house, roast beef, turkey and dressing, mashed potatoes and gravy, and pies of all kinds. Relatives dropped by, aunts, uncles, and cousins, some of whom I hadn't seen since last Christmas. We sat together and ate, exchanged gifts, played cards in the kitchen until late in the evening, and we laughed and ate some more. Our Christmases of the fifties and sixties were very merry indeed.

Throughout the day, friends and neighbors stopped by to wish us a Merry Christmas. They didn't knock. They just came in as if they were family. And in many ways, they were.

Then, all too soon, it was back to school. Christmas vacation was over.

Chapter 13
Dillenbeck School

E veryone has heard tales of walking to school through snow and rain, two miles uphill both ways. Well, I don't know how true such stories are, but school today is very different from school in the 1950's. For one thing, there were no computers or calculators. For another, children didn't talk back to teachers. Moreover, parents didn't side with their children over teachers, but insisted that we "toe the mark." If we found ourselves in trouble at school, we found double trouble at home.

Dillenbeck was a red brick schoolhouse with two classrooms. Grades, one through four, shared one room, fifth through eighth the other. Large windows lined the outer walls allowing light to enter and us to look out.

An oil furnace in one corner of the basement heated the building, but the greater portion of the basement served as our auditorium, complete with stage and elaborate hand-painted curtain. The curtain rolled up and down and was a wonderful example of American folk-art with its central mural design surrounded by local business advertisements.

Maps and pictures of presidents and historic events were evident around the classrooms, while an American flag stood proudly in one corner. Our school day opened with the Pledge of Allegiance; a practice I think should continue in classrooms today.

Above the blackboards and running across the front of the room was an example of the alphabet in both upper and lowercase letters.

This exhibited the "Palmer Method" of penmanship and, using foolscap paper, we regularly practiced the push-pull strokes peculiar to this technique. Not that I developed good penmanship, but that was the goal.

We typically used flash cards too, especially for math problems. Flash cards were simply pieces of paper with problems written on and shown to you randomly. The challenge was to calculate the solution quickly. You couldn't just learn by rote, not unless you had an unusually good memory. Therefore, you actually learned how to do math in your head.

I began school just after turning six. Like the other kids, I carried sack lunches to school. Mine were very simple, sweet things usually, certainly not the sort recommended for schoolchildren today. Oftentimes my sandwiches were made with bread, butter and brown sugar, or sometimes powdered sugar. Later, Mom packed sandwiches of peanut butter and maple syrup. Occasionally I snacked on graham crackers.

Dillenbeck School had no running water, so we pumped our drinking water from a well next to the building. Each day at recess, and again during lunch, children lined up at the well for their turn to get a drink.

Honeybees visited the pump to get water for their hive. When they landed on the edge of a perpetual puddle near the pump, my friend

Schultzie and I would catch them by hand to show off. We were rarely stung. We simply cupped our hands around the bee slowly, trapping it. Sometimes we picked one up by the wings. That was more exciting because they buzzed when they struggled to free themselves, and when they tried to sting, their stingers usually struck only our fingernails instead of skin. I say "usually."

With no running water, of course we had outhouses. They too were on the side of the building, within fifty feet of the well. Today the well and outhouses could never be in such close proximity. Perhaps we were tougher then, or not as knowledgeable.

The Johnson sisters, Esther and Ruth, were our teachers. My teacher, Esther, made us raise our hand for permission to use the outhouse during class. We had to hold up one or two fingers, the number of fingers indicating what we had to do. Why it was important for her to know that, I never learned.

One day I was ill and had to make repeated trips to the outhouse. My teacher allowed me to go two or three times, before she became upset, announcing aloud in front of the class, "If you ask to go out one more time, I'm going to come out and watch you." She evidently didn't understand my discomfort or didn't care. I struggled miserably through the remainder of the day. This was my first, but by no means my last encounter with a domineering and unjust "authority figure."

Not all of my teachers were like her. The next teacher I had was Mr. Burris. He was a very good teacher, but he enjoyed hunting raccoons and was easily sidetracked by questions about hunting. Sometimes the older boys got him to talk about his dogs and, well, it was as if school was over for the day, for once he started talking about his adventures in the field, he could go on for hours.

During recess, everyone went outside to play. Dillenbeck had slides, rings, swings, a merry-go-round and teeter-totter. When we played on the teeter-totter, we boys didn't simply go up and down. Instead, we pushed off with such force as to make the other person fly dangerously high.

And swings allowed us to soar in long high arcs where we made a game of seeing who could jump the farthest. Rarely was anyone hurt doing this. The only injury I remember was when my friend Ronnie fell off the slide, breaking his arm. I can still see him running into the building in pain, clutching his arm.

All the children, young and old, played together on the merry-go-round, a large affair suspended from heavy steel rods. On it, we not only spun around but sometimes simultaneously swung from side to side. Younger children held on tightly as the older ones gave them a thrilling spin.

Other games, like pom-pom pull-away, also allowed young and old to play together. To play this, we divided into two teams, each team linking arms and facing their opponents across a large playing field. One-by-one, someone was challenged to break through the other team's line. If they succeeded, the two who broke the link became members of the other's team. If the line did not break, the one who charged the line became part of it. Play continued in this way until everyone was on a single team so that, in the end, everyone was on the winning team.

Because it was forbidden, passing notes in class was a favorite pastime of mine. As it was a challenge to communicate this way without being caught, and because I planned to be a spy when I grew up, my friend, Bill and I developed a special code.

Using this code, we passed notes back and forth during class, ciphering and deciphering messages, having a great time. We were heedless of being caught, knowing our teacher could never read the notes.

However, we soon became carried away, using stronger language and telling nastier jokes. Finally, in our haste to be funny, we began sending not only the coded message but the decoded one as well.

Then we were caught. The expression on Mr. Burris's face when he read our notes taught me a lesson about being a better spy.

Mrs. Zipze was our music teacher. An older woman, thin with graying hair, she visited Dillenbeck once each week and formed choirs in each classroom. She had each class stand at the front of the room where we lined up according to size to sing patriotic songs and songs of Christmas. I didn't realize there was a purpose behind our singing, but we were practicing for a Christmas program.

At the end of each music lesson, Mrs. Zipze asked if anyone had a favorite song they would like us to sing, and each time I raised my hand, asking to sing *The Marine's Hymn* since my brother Ken was in the Marines. Mrs. Zipze never failed to honor my request, and the class belted out its version of *The Marine's Hymn*, while I sang as loud as any and beamed with pride.

A few weeks before Christmas, our practice took on fresh intensity. Classes were divided into groups to practice their roles in the play. Mrs. Zipze picked a role that called for me to learn a little song, but try as I might, I could not get it right. Finally, Mrs. Zipze gave up.

I still think she had tears in her eyes because I was so hopeless, but maybe she only pretended to cry to convince me that I should do something else. In any case, she gave me a different part in the play, playing a snare drum. As the choir sang "*Little Drummer Boy*" I simply kept time, playing a soft rat-a-tat-tat.

Mrs. Zipze challenged me to take a simple speaking part too. In one scene, a group of children surrounded Santa Claus who, tired from his rounds, had fallen asleep in a chair. Then, as he roused, all the children were directed to run off stage with me being the last one. As I exited, I was to turn around and say to the audience, "Gee! He's a pippin.'"

Finally, the big night arrived. Families filled the room quickly and the beautiful hand-painted curtain rolled up. The pageant we had practiced so hard and long for had begun. I remember little more about the play, except that my rat-a-tat-tat seemed curiously out-of-sync, and that I hurriedly left the stage after the Santa scene failing to give my "Gee! He's a pippin" speech.

We celebrated other holidays at school too. On Valentine's Day, we exchanged cards, many of which were handmade. Everybody got one. No one was to be slighted. Each child decorated a box and put their name on it for the cards. Mom had bought me a packet of valentines to give out, some with silly caricatures, some of friendship. However, I had saved my pennies to buy a card for my latest flame, Marnie. I wanted her to have one that was special.

On the appointed day, we brought our cards to school, dropping them into the boxes. Then we anxiously waited for the end of the day when we could open our boxes to see what our classmates had given us. That was a long day for me. I could hardly wait.

Finally, it was time. With high hopes and anticipation, I opened my box. Quickly looking through my cards, I searched for one from Marnie. Surely, like the one I bought for her, hers would be large and store-bought, gushing with hearts and warm thoughts. But anticipation turned to anguish when I found nothing at all from her.

She must have wanted to give it to me in person, I thought. Or maybe Danny swiped it and threw it away. There had to be an explanation. An oversight? But no. Nothing from Marnie. I hated Valentine's Day.

Late in the school year, shortly before summer vacation, there was an accident near the school. An ice cream truck skidded off the highway and into the ditch. Unhurt, the driver came to our school to seek help in getting his truck out. Mr. Burris and some of the older boys helped push his truck back onto the roadway, and as a reward, everyone was given ice cream treats.

When spring arrived, our thoughts turned to freedom and playing outdoors. Baseball games scheduled between Dillenbeck, and neighboring country schools were more like picnics. We looked forward to these events where many pleasant rivalries and lasting friendships developed.

Chapter 14
Preparations

Ever a planner, I always looked forward to doing things outdoors. Every summer our family vacationed in Wisconsin's north woods. But sometimes we went off, if only for an evening, to fish in local ponds. Such times brought me as much joy as any distant vacation and were just as worthy of the preparation.

Mud oozed between my toes as I made my way in the dark. A dim flashlight with red cellophane taped across its lens was my only light. I stepped carefully so not to alert my prey. The rain had stopped, yet water dripped from trees overhead. An icy drop fell down my neck causing me to shiver.

One hand clutched my light while the other was poised, ready to strike. I knew my quarry was nearby. Clouds lit the night sky as lightning flashed in the distance. The storm was moving off.

I knelt low, scanning the earth for sign as distant thunder rumbled. My flashlight's beam reflected off something in the grass. Instantly I pounced. This nightcrawler was mine!

I sought these giant earthworms for fishing bait. In a single night, I could easily capture several dozen, enough for several fishing expeditions if properly cared for.

My dad had recently built a large wooden box to keep our worms in, burying it level with the ground in a cool corner of our backyard beneath a tree. A hinged lid kept skunks out while a bottom made of window screen allowed rain to escape though not the worms. There is nothing so horrible on a hot summer day as the stench of rotting worms caused by overcrowding or too much moisture.

Nearly everyone in my family pursued nightcrawlers at one time or another. My mother was especially good at catching them, but my Uncle Leslie had his own proven method. He fixed electrical wires to two metal rods that had wooden handles. With an electrical plug at the other end, the wires were plugged in to make one rod positive and the other negative.

Whenever he needed nightcrawlers for fishing, he just watered his lawn thoroughly, plugged his contraption in, pushed the rods into the earth about ten feet apart, and within minutes the ground was littered with writhing worms of all kinds. He had only to unplug the rods and select the worms he wanted. Only once did he fail to unplug his invention first, but that one time was enough to burn the incident indelibly into his memory.

Dad never let me build or use such a device, pointing out its dangers and Uncle Les' narrow escape. But I didn't mind. My method worked well enough and provided challenges and even a certain measure of adventure, much like fishing itself.

Willie's Pond provided a wonderful fishing adventure. For a small fee, one could catch enough bullheads to fill a bucket or a boat. The pond was five miles north of Janesville. These were always exciting times as we eagerly anticipated Dad driving us there in his old Kaiser automobile, our bamboo fishing poles lashed to the door handles. Once there, my folks and I, my brothers and sister, and even my grandmother enjoyed many an evening sitting on the grassy bank of the pond or in a rented rowboat, drifting nightcrawlers across the bottom for bullheads.

Grandma loved to fish. We never had to wonder who had one on when it was she. Her screams told us. "Oh! I've got one! Donny. Come here. Take him off for me would you" she said, as she held the shiny, writhing creature in the air. I gladly removed them for her, holding the fish gingerly, taking care to hold it just right because getting pricked by the spines of a bullhead can be very painful.

Grandma wasn't afraid to take her own fish off her hook, or to bait it either. She just liked it when she could get one of us to do it for her.

But our trips to Willie's Pond were only a prelude to the real thing, our big trip "up north" to Birchwood where we stayed in a cabin at my Uncle Lester's resort on Birch Lake. There, at his Echo Bay Resort, I could fish all day and night.

Such trips were the highlight of my summers and I planned for months before them, gathering my fishing tackle, what little I had, cleaning and organizing, sharpening hooks, oiling reels, and making setlines to place around the shoreline or between the many stumps in the bays, a practice illegal today.

To make setlines, I wrapped fifty to a hundred feet of heavy casting line onto makeshift spools. Adding a series of hooks and sinkers to the line, I placed minnows or large nightcrawlers on the hooks. Then I placed the setlines in likely spots and returned every few hours to see if I had a northern pike or fat bullhead. Anticipation of such exploits motivated my planning.

The thought of fishing and my planning for these trips provided me with hours of pleasure, although a previous experience with setlines wasn't so pleasurable. My brother Chuck was making one, attaching hooks to a long string he had tied between two trees in front of our cabin. Unaware that it was there, I ran down the hill and smacked into it. Next thing I knew, I was lying on my back, looking up. Then I realized a fishhook was dangling from my mouth.

Mom asked Uncle Lester to help take it out. He was experienced in extracting fishhooks and promptly snipped the barb off with a pliers, drawing the hook out painlessly. A quick trip to town for a tetanus shot and I was good as new and ready to fish again.

It was thoughts such as these of fishing that drew me out in the rain late at night to catch as many nightcrawlers as I could, for soon it would be time again for vacation, to go up north.

Chapter 15
Chicken Beaks and Rattlesnakes

B oys, both young and old, have always needed to feel important. Combine that need with an active imagination and you might create adventure from the simplest of things, even a dead chicken.

I am amazed how some people believe only what they want, refusing to change their minds even after being shown proof. Closed minded, that's what they are. And it's a shame too. Just think what they could be, what they could learn, if only they would listen, especially if they listened to someone like me.

Mr. Hendrickson lived on Black Bridge Road, a block away, next door to Schultzie. He raised chickens behind his house, providing meat and eggs for his and several other families. When they were grown, he butchered them in his back yard.

One of my favorite places to play was the field behind his house. Fields back then often had no fences, just wide strips of grass or brush separating each field. That's what I liked about the fields back then. Those natural borders between the fields provided habitat for wildlife and protection from erosion, but more than that, they also provided places for adventure for kids like me.

On those narrow strips of wilderness, we exercised our imaginations, hunted birds with B-B guns, and rabbits with homemade bows and arrows. Old, weathered stumps lurked in the brush waiting to pounce upon some unsuspecting boy, though we bravely fought them off with our ready-made spears of horseweed handily jerked from the ground.

Schultzie and I found a skull behind Mr. Hendrickson's home one day. Bleached white by the sun, it was small, about two inches long and one inch wide. The eye-sockets were very prominent. There was no brow, and the crown was very round.

However, most intriguing to us amateur anatomists, was the mandible. The lower jaw of course was missing. But the upper looked strange to us, consisting of two long, thin bones that began at the cheeks, ran forward and curved gently downward. They nearly joined in a point about one inch from their beginning. Much like teeth. More like fangs. Fangs! Of course, that's what it was. A rattlesnake skull!

Excitedly, we searched for more of the skeleton to verify our hypothesis. What we found was even better. More skulls. Dozens of them, in fact.

Unbelievable! How could so many snake skulls be here, we wondered, when rattlesnakes were so rare in this part of the country? Maybe there was a mass migration, we theorized, and because they were in a part of Wisconsin where they do not occur naturally, they died. Certainly, that was it. It was obvious to us. We were so clever.

Taking our findings, we showed the other kids in the neighborhood, expecting to astonish them with our discovery. Many were impressed. We looked like heroes to them, but not to Shirley.

Shirley was Mr. Hendrickson's daughter, who with a cynical voice simply said, "Chickens."

"Chickens? What do you mean, chickens?" I shot back. "These are rattlesnake skulls."

Shirley asked where we found them. I told her, in the field behind her house. "Chickens," she repeated smugly. To her, just because we found the skulls behind her dad's chicken coop that was proof enough that these were not rattlesnakes. Evidently, she believed, like so many skeptics today, that nothing that unusual is likely to happen to them.

Her mind was made up. And nothing we could say would make her change her mind. Some people are like that.

Chapter 16
The Birds and the Bees

Drugs, shootings, wild music and punk hair would make me want to cloister my kids if I had to raise them today. I'd be a nervous wreck. And sex? Why, today kids know more about sex in grade school than I knew when I got married. Sex follows kids to school, fills their music, is seen on television and advertising... it's everywhere. Why can't kids learn about sex the way we did, on the street, where it belongs.

In America today, nothing is taboo. Any topic, any kind of language, any action is not only talked about, but seems to be practiced. When I was a boy, this just wasn't so. The strong language so commonly used today, while not unheard of in my generation, was more carefully used. It was doled out, so to speak, as it seemed necessary, like when your finger got caught in your bicycle's spokes. The use of strong language carried more influence then because it was more judiciously used, and it was rarely used around the opposite sex.

While kids today feel their hormones jumping about inside them at the age of ten or twelve, it was no different for our generation. The difference today is that kids are taught what those urges mean, and they tend to act on them. We just thought we were weird. For a ten-year-old in the 1950s, to be sexually active meant having played "Doctor."

I hadn't given any real thought to the difference between boys and girls until one summer day when I was innocently playing in front of my home. While throwing rocks at the neighbor's cat or something, two of my friends, Bud and John, rode up to me on their bikes. Their expressions told me they had something important on their minds. They did. They looked first to the left, then to the right, making sure the coast was clear, then they asked in hushed tones if I knew where babies came from.

"Sure" I lied, "Doesn't everybody?"

"Come on," Bud said, "let's take a ride and we'll tell you all about it."

These two older boys had always been good for an adventure of one kind or another, so I didn't hesitate. I jumped on my sister's bicycle and rode with them down the Black Bridge Road where it was safe to talk.

When we reached the sandpit, we stopped. They looked around to be sure no one was within earshot. Again, I was asked, "Where do you think babies come from?" Well, before I could come up with a good explanation for this mystery, they described to me some outlandish process.

Well, I was astounded. I never imagined. I was dumbfounded. Nearly speechless, I said, "I knew that." Then, in silence, I rode back home to contemplate this new turn of events.

This news did seem to explain a few things though, like why only women got big bellies from swallowing watermelon seeds. Or why it was women again, who got such big "beer bellies" when it was the men in our neighborhood who did most of the drinking. And this powerful bit of knowledge made playing "Doctor" a whole new game for me.

I met her at the Dillenbeck School, and I can still see her dark hair and dimples, her sparkling eyes and smile. Marilyn lived two blocks away, yet somehow, I didn't know her until I started school. This was probably because she didn't associate with the kids I played with. But once she caught my attention, I did everything I could to catch hers. I needn't have tried so hard.

Marilyn was a pretty little girl and was very bright. I was just a towheaded boy with a silly grin and ears that stuck out. She was polite and mature. I was immature, both physically and mentally. Her father was a cabinetmaker, a craftsman. My dad roofed houses and barns. Her home was, although not elaborate, certainly well kept, while my home had its beginnings as a walk-in freezer. Marilyn was the third of three and I was the fourth of four children. But, beyond our both being the youngest in our families, we had nothing else in common.

I was shy around girls, never knowing what to say, so naturally, if I spoke at all, I only said something stupid. This has never changed. Though I couldn't force myself to talk to her, I wanted very badly to be noticed by her, to have her like and admire me. Consequently, I did things to get her to see me, unaware that I was just making a fool of myself. In this endeavor, I had friends who were only too glad to help.

Ron and Mike were especially helpful. Together, the three of us went, not to her home, but near enough where she could see me, and there we wrestled and fought, with me of course, winning every battle. The object was to show her how strong I was, how brave I was. I won many battles before her, but not the battle for her. But then, good grief, I was only seven!

Then when I grew up and was eight, Marnie moved into our neighborhood. She lived but a few houses away. Marnie was two years older than me and went to the same school. She was tall and auburn haired, and I liked her right away, though she didn't know I was alive. Marnie wanted an older man, someone more like Danny.

Danny was Marnie's age, but I had figured out a way to win her over and do it in a very mature and respectable way. I would scare Danny away.

Danny was six inches taller than I and much larger. With me being a skinny little kid, whose largest features were his ears, I couldn't hope to beat him up and take her away. But I did come up with a plan that was near perfect. I wrote a letter of such force and brutality that Danny would be afraid to continue seeing her, thus delivering her over to me.

I wrote the letter on a piece of paper torn from a grocery sack, part of my plan to prevent its being traced to me. On it I wrote, "Leave her alone. She's mine!" and at the bottom I signed it, "The Blob," making an impressive inkblot as only "The Blob" could, showing how serious I was.

The next day I stayed inside while the other kids went outside for recess. While the others were playing, I slipped my note into Danny's desk. After recess, I was at my desk when Danny entered the room. I watched as he opened his desk and saw my note.

Acting nonchalant, I hid behind my reader, waiting for Danny to read the note from "The Blob." Smiling to myself, I imagined his face turning white with horror. I expected him to become frightened, pack his clothes, and leave town.

Danny saw the note and picked it up. I watched his expression as he read. What I saw wasn't quite what I had hoped for. He smiled. Then he showed it to Marnie whose desk was next to his. From the corner of my eye, I watched as they talked animatedly and looked at me. Then, together they rose from their desks and came my way.

I pretended to pour over my studies as if I was unaware of their presence when Danny dropped the note in front of me asking, "Did you write this?" Feigning innocence, I looked at it and denied ever having seen it, or of owning an ink pen, or of having grocery bags at home on which to write such dribble. With beads of moisture forming on my brow, I denied everything. And I wasn't really lying, merely being prudent. And they must have believed me, because Danny told me what he would do to the guy who wrote it if he ever caught him, and I'm still alive.

This didn't stop my attempts to win Marnie over. It only set my plans back a bit. The following summer, I tried again.

Marnie's family had a small vegetable garden bordering the street near her home and Marnie tended this garden regularly. The street was being prepared for paving, and yet was merely gravel. Conveniently, a three-foot high mound of gravel lay in a pile directly across from her garden. This provided me with a way, not only to get Marnie to notice me, but to impress her by showing off my skill and daring. I simply had to wait for the right opportunity. Finally, that opportunity arrived.

Looking around the street corner one warm and sunny Saturday, I saw Marnie hoeing weeds from the garden. Not wasting a minute lest my opportunity slip away, I jumped on my bicycle to carry out my plan. Rapidly, I pedaled down the gravel road toward my objective, the gravel mound. Marnie was still working in her garden, facing the road. As I neared the mound, I quickened my pace and braced myself. My bike and I went up the mound of gravel and together we sailed, coming down on the other side, a jump of a good ten feet.

I looked to see if Marnie was marveling at my daring feat, but she had turned and missed my bravery. So once again, I had to leap over that mound. This time I rode even faster than before and again I flew with my bike in a graceful and impressive arc, through the air, jumping farther than before, coming down in the gravel road with a hard thump. Surely, that would impress her, I thought. But again Marnie seemed to have missed seeing me.

"How could she not see that?" I wondered. "That was such a great leap, nearly suicidal, and such a great landing."

Frustrated now, I pedaled toward the mound again, this time with more determination than ever. Faster and faster, I pedaled, hitting and leaping over the pile of gravel, soaring through the air... coming down... sideways! In a cloud of dust and bicycle parts, I tumbled down the gravel road.

When I regained enough sense to remember what had happened, I imagined Marnie would be kneeling over me, trying to comfort me in my pain. But when I opened my eyes, I saw she wasn't able to help me. She had all she could do to stand up herself, she was laughing so hard. That was when I realized what real pain is.

As I reached my teens, I began to pay more attention to girls. Penny was a year or two younger than I, but already she was developing into quite a young woman. Not long ago, she was just another neighbor, like one of the guys. But now, I had noticed, almost like mushrooms, she had blossomed overnight.

Penny was at the Marty's, talking with Marsha and Mary, younger sisters of Marnie, my old flame. When I came walking down the road they called to me, giggling as girls do. Thinking nothing of it, I stopped to talk.

Penny was wearing short shorts and a halter-top that was equally short. As she spoke, very animatedly, her halter rode up in a most interesting way and she had to tug and pull it back down frequently. I couldn't help but notice, and the girls were delighted in watching me notice.

"Well, I can't help it. It just keeps doing that," she said, pulling her halter back down again and smiling as she did so.

I squirmed while Mary and Marsha delighted in my discomfort, hardly able to keep from laughing.

Whether Penny had outgrown her halter top or if she deliberately wore one that was too small, I had no idea. Nor did I care.

Then Mrs. Marty came from the house, joining us. It didn't take her but a few moments to see what was happening and proceeded to scold me for staring, for it was obvious what I was watching.

Red-faced, I stammered, "Huh? But I...We...I didn't...We were just..."

"I know what you were doing. And I know what she's doing too. And I think you all better go home."

Therefore, I left, completely forgetting where it was, I was going originally.

Later that summer, I lay in bed reading comic books and listening to the radio. My folks were in bed as was my sister Karen. My brother, Chuck, was out on a date and not expected to be home until late.

Something strange caught my eye, a shadow or something, faintly moving against the bedroom wall. I watched it for a minute before realizing it wasn't a shadow but a light. I turned off my bedroom light and it became clear that someone was shining a light through my bedroom window from outside.

When I looked out my window, a shadowy form shined a light in my face. I recognized the form. Penny.

"C'mon out," she whispered. I waved and slipped on my blue jeans, then sneaked quietly down the stairs. Tiptoeing through the kitchen, I went out the back door and there stood Penny beside our garage in her Teddy Bear pajamas.

"What're you doing out here," I asked.

"I saw your light was on," she said, "and I couldn't sleep. Just thought you might want to talk."

Talking wasn't all that was on my mind, although I didn't really know how to do anything else.

"Yeah. Sure," I said. "Whatcha wanta talk about?" I was smooth like that with the girls.

We sat in the dark beside the garage, watching stars by the billions overhead. A chorus of crickets chirped while we talked late into the warm summer night.

Then Penny said, "I'm getting chilly," and before I could suggest she might want to go inside, she slid close to me. The warmth of her body made me break into a sweat.

"Whoa!" I thought, "Am I a lady's man or what?"

Just then, car lights lit the driveway. Chuck! Penny ducked low while I was caught in the glare. Turning off his lights, Chuck got out of the car as I stood up and walked toward him.

"What're you doing out here?" he asked.

"Lookin' for nightcrawlers," I lied.

"You got a pail to put them in?"

"Left it over there. Haven't found very many."

"Where's your flashlight?"

"It's over there too."

"Un-huh. Well, I'm going to bed," he said, heading toward the house.

Glancing over my shoulder, I saw Penny going into her house too. She waved.

"Well, guess I'll go to bed then too," I said, ending my first late-night rendezvous.

She and I met a couple more times that summer, talking and sitting close. Each time I thought myself to be a lady's man while she probably thought I was something else.

Another favorite meeting place for couples was the Little League ballpark on the edge of our neighborhood. The dugouts made an ideal place to meet. Dark and shadowy, we could see anyone coming from far off.

Our routine was to meet at the community water pump after dark and take a circuitous route to the Little League Park. The route was important, because we didn't want people to know our destination.

Sometimes two or three couples met there, in which case little more occurred than quiet talking and mild teasing. But other times a couple might be the only ones there. When that happened, the results were the same, only the reporting of the activities was exaggerated.

Reports were important to boys, affecting one's status within the hierarchy. My reports were either unimpressive or unbelievable. Consequently, my status as a lady's man never climbed very high, thus pretty much reflecting reality.

"Hi, ya Babe."

"What?"

"Hi, Babe."

"Am I a 'Babe?'"

"Well..."

"Where'd you come up with that, 'Hi Babe stuff?'"

"That's what my brother would say, so I figured, that's what I'd say."

"Hi, Babe, yourself. Sit down. The movie's gonna start."

It was a Saturday, and I was meeting Barb at the matinee. Her friend Linda was with her.

In school, Barb told me she would be coming to the movies, so we agreed to meet. My first date. At least, I saw it as a date.

Barb was in my grade in school and was very outgoing and friendly. I took her friendliness for "liking," so I "liked" her in return.

We met at the movies several times that summer, sometimes in the balcony of the Meyers Theater, sometimes out front as we waited in line for tickets. We always went "Dutch," buying our own ticket. Still, I thought of these meetings as "dates."

Having embarrassed myself on our first meeting by saying "Hi, Babe," I was no more mature on subsequent "dates." Still, she tolerated my *faux pas* well and our friendship endured, even if it didn't grow. Nonetheless, I was learning how to conduct myself with the opposite sex.

I had a lot to learn.

Bud said to me, "Hey. You want to know how to get a girl's attention, just say to her, 'How they hangin'."

"What?"

"Yeah. Just ask her, 'How they hangin?' If she says to you, 'One down one side, one down the other,' you got it made in the shade. But watch out if she says, 'Two to a bunch.' If she says that, look out 'cause she's mad about somethin'."

"Yeah?"

"Yeah. Just try it. Say it to the next girl you see and see what she says."

"But what does it mean?" I asked.

"Huh?"

"What does it mean, 'How they hanging?'"

"Well – Don't you know?"

"No. What does it mean? Why would a girl get mad?"

"Well – I don't know either. But they know what it means. It works. Just try it. You'll see."

Thus, my sex education continued.

Chapter 17
A Day on the Road

A *boy growing up in the 1950's rarely complained of having nothing to do. There was always something. Whether fishing, playing or just discovering, he was up early and home late. That is, if he had the freedom allowed by my parents. And most parents did allow more freedom then. Why not? Life was more innocent. Kids were less apt to do something to get into trouble because they were too busy discovering life. Or were they?*

I awoke early, my bedroom curtains blowing gently on a soft summer breeze that carried with it birdsong and the promise of adventure. I got out of my bed and looked out the window. From there, from the second floor of our family home, I could see much of my neighborhood. Behind our back yard and to my right, partly hidden by brush and trees was Old John's shack. Apple trees nearly surrounded a home to my left. From the other window I saw Bud's and Ron's, and several other homes. The red roof of Mike's house peeked through the trees in the distance.

I heard familiar sounds; people talking, Mom fixing breakfast, a tractor cultivating a field across the road from our home. One familiar sound was missing though, that of the gravel quarry. Usually sounds from the digging and screening equipment and the conveyor carried the half-mile to our home. Today though, it was conspicuously absent. Then I remembered. This was Saturday and Schultzie and I had planned to spend the day exploring together.

Dressing quickly, I hurried downstairs. Dad was pouring catsup over his fried potatoes and eggs while Mom buttered his toast. I took a large bowl and filled it with Sugar Crisps® and milk. Mom knew I had a busy day planned when I used a large bowl for my cereal rather than having several smaller bowls. This was my way of saving time when I was in a hurry.

Knowing I probably would not be home for lunch, she asked, "Where are you off to today?"

"Down the road with Schultzie," I answered. Then I darted out the door.

Mom seldom had to fix me much, especially at breakfast. As long as we had milk and Sugar Crisps®, I had all I needed to start my day.

Schultzie was waiting for me in front of his home. He was always ready for adventure.

"Set to go?" I asked.

"I'm ready. Been ready. What kept ya?"

It was after 8 o'clock and much of the morning had passed already. Across the road from Schultzie's, Jimmy and Ted, neighbors of Schultzie called out to us. They were playing in the vacant lot, so we joined them. They were climbing spindly saplings, box elder trees fifteen to twenty feet tall that had sprouted around an old foundation. This foundation was all that remained of an old farmstead, abandoned long ago. It was places like that that were among our favorites to play.

We played lumberjack, chopping down some of the weedy trees and like monkeys, we climbed others playing Tarzan. We had great fun swaying from some of the larger trees, with trunks three or four inches in diameter, daring one another to go from one tree to the next, seeing who could travel the furthest by treetop. The spindliest trees were most fun to climb as they sagged from our weight as we climbed until they bent to the ground.

Then Schultzie said to me, "Let's go to the pit," meaning the sandpit down the road.

"I'm with you," I agreed and in a short while we were standing at the edge of the pit, looking over the sloping sides to the ponds below. There we saw a long snake-like conveyor belt that transported the gravel from the pit to a concrete block plant a quarter mile away.

A crane for digging gravel and a large hopper for loading the gravel onto the conveyor were within throwing distance. Sometimes when the quarry was being mined, we tested our throwing arms by tossing stones down onto the crane hitting it with a resounding clang.

"Betcha can't hit that can down there," I said, pointing to a gas can floating on the largest pond.

"I'll hit it before you can," Schultzie replied, and the contest was on.

Throwing rocks at targets was a regular challenge for us. One after another, our stones sailed out over the pit in long and graceful arcs. They fell down, down, down until finally hitting the water with a splash that sent plumes high into the air like a bomb in a war movie. Pretending we were firing cannons at enemy ships; we watched as concentric circles spread outward from our shelling.

The sides of the pit sloped at a steep angle in most spots, and in some places dropped straight down for thirty or forty feet before beginning to slope. At places like that, we threw stones against the vertical sides producing small avalanches until eventually, after repeated stoning, the sides eroded, and tons of material broke loose.

"Hey, lookit that," Schultzie said, pointing at a series of cracks near the edge. Here, vast amounts of gravel were about to give way. All that was needed was the proper stimulation, which we were happy to provide. Walking along these edges, we kicked at the cracks with one foot and leaped back rapidly. In this way, we caused gravel slides of various sizes, frequently many tons of material. A few times, we found ourselves dropping with the gravel unable to react quickly enough to jump clear. But being atop the gravel instead of below it, we always managed to ride the slide safely.

There were two large concrete structures halfway across the pit. Once used in the process of sorting or transferring gravel into trucks or conveyors, they were long ago abandoned. Standing out of kilter, they looked like two huge cinder blocks left tossed upon the sand. We speculated that they must have been above the pit at one time, then as the great pit grew and the gravel was dug from beneath, they finally tumbled in, sliding to where they now rested.

Surrounded by brush and small trees that grew up around them, many kids enjoyed playing in and around these fortresses. They made great hiding places and provided exercise for our imaginations. One day they might be ships on a tossing sea, another day caverns, but every day they provided adventure.

To get inside them, we would climb through a hole where a gravel chute had once been. Inside it was quiet and peaceful amid the shady coolness of the thick concrete. A shallow pool of water stood in one corner. Algae and tadpoles in the pool provided many lessons for us. There we observed life and death in one of the many environs encountered on our adventures.

Since it was Saturday and no one was working in the quarry, Schultzie said, "Let's take a look around."

"Lead the way," I said, and in the next moment we were skipping down the steep bank, taking ten and fifteen-foot bounds. Rocks rolled and gravel rattled as we raced each other to the bottom and dust rose like a cloud around us. Schultzie, as usual, got there first. Looking back up, we saw sheets of gravel sliding where we had come down, like a slow-motion avalanche.

Once at the bottom of the quarry we looked into the nearest pond. Like the others, it was two to six feet deep and had sparse vegetation around the edge. Few plants could grow in the sterile, desert-like conditions of the sandpit.

Sneaking carefully to the edge of the pond, we saw bass, bluegills and suckers swimming in the crystalline waters. We wondered how they got there, whether they were introduced by workers at the quarry or brought in as eggs on the feet and feathers of birds. Either way, they obviously thrived in the seclusion of the sandpit.

Suckers darted off at our approach, but the bluegills were less concerned. And bass, some of impressive size, cruised slowly in formation like a squadron of submarines. "Hey. We got to come back here sometime," I said, and Schultzie and I immediately made plans for a return trip, next time bringing our fishing poles.

Dragonflies danced above the water as we walked around the edge of the pond Turtles basked in the sunshine looking like shiny rocks until we got too close. Then they leaped into the clear water to escape. I watched one as it swam gracefully away, legs pulling at the water with alternating strokes. He swam but a short distance, and then he stopped as if frozen. Unmoving, he eyed us for a long while, and then slowly rose to the surface with hardly a movement. His nose broke the surface of the water where he took a quick breath and dove again, swimming farther away, disappearing amid some underwater weeds. From previous experience, I knew that turtles, when they feel safe, simply swim off slowly to feed or to bask in the sun. This one evidently felt threatened by our presence.

Frogs hopped into the water as we walked along the edge of the pond. "There goes our bass bait," Schultzie said. Frogs make great bait for bass and there was an abundance of them here.

Nearing the conveyor belt, I suggested we climb onto it for easier walking. The belt stood five or six feet high and was fully four feet wide. It was very heavy, perhaps three-quarters of an inch thick. Climbing onto the now-still conveyor, we followed it in the direction of the factory.

Here we had a better view of the pit. To my left, I saw a high wall of gravel, barren and stark, sloping at a steep angle. Ahead was the factory. Between the factory and us loomed the two massive concrete structures. On my right, the wall of the pit was wooded and undulating. It was here that we liked to exit the pit, near the railroad tracks.

Behind me, toward the Black Bridge Road, rose the highest wall. Bands of color showed various strata where gravel had amassed over the ages. One could hardly imagine the measureless time that had passed in accumulating to such depths the sand and gravel I was looking at, topped with a layer of gray clay and rich, black earth. Yet, here was evidence of that time. The layer of clay and earth at the top, with its thin green band of grass and shrubs, represented the time since the last glacier. How much time did the layers of gravel represent? This was part of my adventure and education.

A culvert protruded from the high wall, its end hanging out over the pit, some fifteen or twenty feet below the rim, a culvert I would one day foolishly dare to crawl into. From the end of the culvert, water trickled, falling over a hundred feet to the rocks below.

"Whatcha say we go down the tracks?" Schultzie said. The railroad tracks were just a couple hundred yards away.

"OK by me," I said, as we climbed down from the conveyor. Crossing the floor of the pit, we saw a remarkable variety of rock, ranging from caramel brown mudstone and red granite, to sandstone and milky quartz. We were watchful for common limestone too, which often contained fossilized coral and seashells.

"Hey. Lookit this one," I said to Schultzie, showing him a piece of mudstone. A creamy white seashell was imbedded in it. "I'm gonna add this to my collection."

Schultzie admired the rock and handed it back to me, and then we continued on our way.

We came to the railroad tracks where they passed the city dump where we often searched for treasures. Beyond the dump loomed the smokestack of the Parker Pen Company.

"What's that up ahead," Schultzie said, pointing to a half-spent railroad flare beside some bushes. "Looks like a good one."

We were always alert for railroad flares. They provided important ingredients for the rocket fuels we made, mixing the contents of flares with gunpowder, a very dangerous practice. Sometimes we just lit the flares at night to watch them burn with their red-orange flame.

Ahead of us, the Black Bridge framed the railroad tracks that curved gently to the left, seeming to meet in the distance. On either side of the tracks the earth rose and spread out like a green carpeted valley as shrubbery shrouded the ravine. Above all this was a cloudless, deep blue summer sky.

We could never be sure where our adventures might take us. Starting with one place in mind, we always ran the risk of being sidetracked before we got there. But that was the fun of it. That was what made our time together an adventure.

Reaching the bridge, Schultzie suggested we head to the archery range, so we climbed the steep bank to see who might be there.

To our right was a second quarry, one abandoned long ago, where "honey trucks" now dumped their loads. A trail beside this foul-smelling place led us to another old concrete structure whose use was similar to those of the other pit. But this one, instead of looking like a huge concrete block, looked more like a giant table whose massive top was supported by four pillars. In the center of the top was a hole about two-foot square where gravel once poured into dump trucks parked beneath.

"Wanna climb up there?" Schultzie asked. "You can see a long way."

"How we gonna get up?" I asked.

"See those?" he said, pointing to some metal reinforcing rods that stuck out from one of the pillars. "I got up there last week with them."

"Follow me," he said as he started to climb.

It wasn't a difficult climb until we reached the top. There we had to pull ourselves over the edge by hanging onto some of the vegetation that had taken root there. But Schultzie was right. We had a grand view of the surrounding pit.

We saw trees, shrubs, grasses and wildflowers in every direction. Downtown, church steeples towered high above the trees that lined the river valley. In the opposite direction, near the horizon, large fuel oil tanks loomed. Nearby, a mound of fine sand lay piled, spilling over the edge of the second pit. This was the only area free of vegetation.

"Wanna check out the ponds?" Schultzie asked, meaning the two ponds that lay at the bottom of this abandoned sandpit.

"Sure," I said. The ponds were always full of life and changed with the seasons, and I enjoyed seeking any new things we might discover.

We found that getting down from our lofty perch was far more difficult than the climb up. In climbing up, we had the advantage of being able to see what to hang onto. When we tried to go down, we had to lie on our bellies and grasp the vegetation while sliding our legs over the edge, blindly seeking footholds. One mistake meant a certain and deadly fall.

Fortunately, we made it down without incident. Then we followed a trail to the bottom of the pit. Long and winding like a serpent, it wound to the bottom, ending between two small ponds.

Trees and shrubs had long since reclaimed the abandoned pit making it an ideal home for rabbits and pheasants. Birdlife abounded here, and we oftentimes caught snakes whenever we could. It was a mystery to us how some people were repelled or frightened by snakes. They were not "slimy" as some people think but dry and, if they have been sunning, warm to the touch.

The ponds teemed with life. A painted turtle basked in the dappled sunlight at the edge of the pond. Searching the pond for frogs, we saw tadpoles and minnows swimming among the vegetation. Redwing blackbirds clung to the cattails and tall reeds on one end of the larger pond, trilling amid a symphony of other bird sounds.

Then we heard a loud boom! The rattle of leaves told us what was happening. Someone was target practicing. This was a common thing to do, to come to the pit and throw clay pigeons, tin cans, or bottles out over the edge, and shoot at them with a shotgun. What we heard rattling on the leaves were pellets from the shotgun blasts as they lost energy and fell around us.

The shooters evidently didn't know we were in the pit, or they wouldn't have been shooting over us. It was unlikely they could see us through all the trees. We weren't overly concerned however, for we had had pellets drop around us before without injury. By the time they reached us, they had little more force than grains of sand.

Still, Schultzie and I decided to move on. To stay away from the shooting, we climbed the north side of the pit instead of taking the trail we entered on. This was more difficult, and we had to pull ourselves up the steep slope by holding onto whatever plants we could grip. Eventually we reached the top. Looking back across the pit we saw three men and a boy, the target shooters. One man tossed clay pigeons while the other two men took turns shooting. The young boy stood watching, certainly wishing he was old enough to join in.

It was afternoon by now, so we decided to start back home. After crossing a bean field, we entered a hay field where we once challenged each other in a foolish game of "chicken."

It was autumn then and the grass was tall and dry. We lay in the dry grass and tossed lit matches between us to see how close each would let the fire get before one of us "chickened out" and moved.

A rooster pheasant cackled ahead of us. A pheasant's call is distinctive, often giving it away as he leaps into the air to escape. A smarter bird would simply fly, making a silent escape that might go unnoticed. But this one ran from cover ahead of us scurrying fifty feet or so, then stopping. Looking back at us, his brightly colored head gleamed in the afternoon sun.

The pheasant continued to run ahead until he reached the end of the field. Unable to go any further without crossing open ground, he waited in the tall grass until we came near. Then he burst into flight with a loud Graaack! Kuk! Kuk! Kuk! and sailed away to safety.

Schultzie and I climbed fences that separated each field, while birds by the hundreds fluttered in the brush. The brush and grasses that lined the fencerows provided prime habitat for a variety of wildlife while today's fields provide little protection for the many birds and animals that once were so plentiful.

The sun was low in the west as our neighborhood came into sight and my stomach told me it was nearly suppertime. So, with a day of exploring behind, Schultzie and I parted, wondering what new adventures tomorrow might bring.

Chapter 18
Annexed

B efore our neighborhood was part of the city, life was innocently simple. Then "progress" hit us, and our world became more complex, and the Boies Addition was never the same.

Annexation meant change. It meant being part of the city. And as part of the city, we had to leave our beloved Dillenbeck school behind. A bus picked us up at the community well and took us to Adams school for one semester, then we were transferred to Roosevelt. That didn't matter, I decided. I didn't like either one. At Dillenbeck, everyone was equal, but in the city schools, kids seemed to be divided according to social classes, rich kids and poor, smart and not so smart, athletes and non-athletes. Yet I didn't feel comfortable in any group.

The last couple of years had been exciting ones for me. Our streets were being paved. A new Woodman's grocery store opened on Milton Avenue and Mount Zion Road and McDonald's opened their first restaurant in town with fifteen-cent hamburgers and twelve-cent fries making competition difficult for the nearby Frostop Drive In. Then Chester Hammes sold Chet's and Dryan's ice cream parlor opened in its place.

Our neighborhood was in the midst of change. Shortly after annexation, sewer, water and gas lines were installed and roads reconstructed, trees were taken down and utility poles moved. Construction on the new interstate highway system had just begun, a project destined to change our nation. And now, this social innovation, the strip mall, Creston Park was opening.

Shopping malls were something new then, a collection of department stores, restaurants and specialty shops away from the downtown. Previously, communities had grown up around industrial and trade centers amid farming areas. Cities, thus, were a collection of neighborhoods surrounding business centers.

Often in these neighborhoods, one found small businesses like the neighborhood taverns and grocery store we had known for so many years. But now there was this new thing, this mall with its variety of stores adjacent to each other with doors that opened under a single shared canopy. A broad sidewalk ran the length of the mall connecting the stores and there was a recessed area with benches and a restaurant.

I had watched the building of this mall for months, and now, finally the "Grand Opening" was underway. A large crowd had gathered. While some people were there for the ribbon cutting ceremony, most awaited the promised giveaways that were to be cast from the back of a large flatbed truck; candy, coupons and prizes, including five live turkeys.

I stood amid the crowd, the largest group of people I had ever seen, with one thing and one thing only on my mind, to get one of the turkeys. It was November 11, 1958, just a week before Thanksgiving, and if my family was to have a Thanksgiving turkey this year, it would be up to me to get it.

Finally, after the long list of speakers wrapped up their remarks, the ribbon was cut, people cheered, and the excitement began.

First, coupons were cast to the crowd, blowing about with people running, pushing and shoving, each trying to get what they could. Then candy rained down, bouncing off heads, shattering on the pavement. Kids, especially, scattered all across the parking lot, eagerly grabbing what they could while I stood watching, my eyes fixed on the five wooden crates holding the turkeys.

That was what I came for. I was eager, yet fearful of disappointment, waiting for my chance. Finally, it came. A large man in blue coveralls opened one of the crates and pulled out a fluttering white turkey. He held it up for all to see, then tossed it into the crowd.

Immediately it was caught. The crowd cheered and awaited another. The next one came and landed on the ground but was quickly surrounded and captured. I was nowhere near either one. I had to move closer.

A third bird was released and was caught by a tall teenager who held it for all to see. With a smile on his face, he took his prize away. Now I grew worried. Three birds released and I wasn't close to any of them.

I shouldered my way closer to the flatbed trailer as the fourth bird was thrown into the air and over my head. Landing among a group of adults, it hit the ground running. Behind it ran young and old, me among them. But before I had gone ten steps, it too was swooped up.

I now stood between those who had chased the bird, and the rest of the crowd. That's when the fifth and last bird was released. It beat its wings in futility, trying desperately to fly. Its trajectory took it toward the mall's stores, toward a recessed cove near the Alpine restaurant.

Being between the buildings and most of the crowd. I raced forward, as did every other kid, but I was ahead of most.

The turkey hit the ground running. I was just twenty yards behind. On either side, other kids raced beside me. With a sudden burst of speed, I raced ahead of the others.

The turkey reached a dead-end. Ahead of the nearest kid by only a couple steps, I grabbed the bird and tucked it beneath my arm like a football. Facing the oncoming mob, I ran back toward them, my free arm stiffly outstretched, like a football player fending off tackles.

Dodging and ducking, I raced through the crowd, past the buildings, across the highway, through my neighborhood, not stopping until I was home. There I proudly displayed my prize to the astonishment and delight of my mother.

Yes, change had come to the Boies Addition. We were now part of the city. Modernization had begun.

Chapter 19
Camping Out

Young boys have always looked forward to "camping out." Whether wanting to face the "monsters" of the darkness or escape other "monsters" at home or if they just wanted to get away from their parents' prying eyes, camping out has always been a highlight of any boy's summer. All of these were good enough reasons for me to want to set up a tent in the backyard.

Butch woke me. It was 4:00 A.M., time to get up. My mind was foggy, and then I remembered we were going fishing. I was fourteen, two years younger than Butch.

I unzipped my sleeping bag and slipped into damp jeans. A train rumbled in the distance, the haunting sound of its twin horns floating across the early morning air. As I tied my shoes, Butch opened the flap and stepped outside.

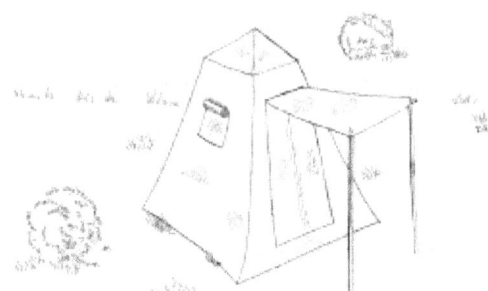

Butch and I were "camping out" in his backyard. We were in my family's two-man mountain tent. Eight feet on each side, it was big enough for two men or four boys. My Uncle Orval left the tent in my care after his last visit. He and his family came to visit us from their home in Texas. He wanted his children to meet some of their relatives and show them where he was born and grew up here in Wisconsin.

After a month of camping and driving around the state, they stopped at our home for a few days. When it came time for them to leave, Uncle Orval asked if he could leave his tent and camping gear with us, so he wouldn't have to haul it back again on their next visit. He said we could use it whenever we wanted. I think it was his way of giving us something that he knew we couldn't afford ourselves because he never camped in Wisconsin again.

We were delighted with his offer, I especially. Before the arrival of that tent, all my camping had been under the stars or beneath a blanket tossed over a clothesline.

Carefully folded, this heavy canvas tent fit snuggly into a military duffel bag with just enough room for its aluminum frame and a bag of stakes. Packed this way, it was all I could manage to carry. We knew nothing of the brightly colored, lightweight nylon tents so popular today. This was U. S. Army surplus in olive drab, but it had a canvas floor, and it was spacious.

"You comin'?" Butch said, as he poked his head back in the tent, his flashlight shining in my eyes.

"Yeah, I'm comin'. Just had to find my jacket."

"Well, c'mon then. Sun'll be up soon."

Stepping onto the dew-covered grass, I looked up at a star-filled sky as Butch disappeared into his house to get our food. The previous day, his mother and sister, Karen, put some things together for our breakfast. Butch's mom broke a dozen eggs into a Tupperware jar and added milk while Karen stuffed a fry pan, spatula, and a few other things into a sack. Butch planned to fry some French toast for us along the riverbank. His mom and sister had seemed as excited about our fishing adventure as we were, laughing and kidding about the fish we would catch.

Butch came back out of the house quietly, so as not to wake anyone. "Here's our grub," he said. "Hop in. Let's get goin'." Butch got his 1948 Chevy when he turned sixteen, removed the chrome, filled in any holes, and painted it a rich metallic green. He took pride in keeping it shiny and running smoothly. I settled in beside him and we were off.

We had shared several adventures already that summer, just one of which was our "camping out." All summer long, we had slept together in that tent, moving it every couple days so as not to kill the grass. Now we were off on another adventure, fishing along the Rock River. Butch had already selected the place we would fish, wanting to get there early enough to beat anyone else.

As we drove, we listened to music from his car radio, a pale-yellow glow coming from the dashboard. Cool morning air swirled through the open windows. As our headlights glowed ahead, I saw a raccoon scramble across the road, and watched as he stared at us from a roadside ditch, his eyes shining as we passed.

"Wanna smoke?" Butch asked, as he lit a cigarette and handed the pack to me.

"Sure, thanks," I said, and took one. Like other boys, I smoked to be "cool." I started smoking when I was eleven, stealing cigarettes from my folks. They always kept a carton or two on a shelf in their bedroom closet where I took what I wanted, making sure to leave the carton to appear as it had before.

A package of cigarettes sold for twenty-five cents and sometimes we "rolled our own" which was cheaper. But I thought free was better yet.

We drove down Black Bridge Road, turning south onto highway 51. Going through the city before dawn, it appeared deserted. Streetlights lit the downtown area, but we didn't see another car.

A few miles farther and Butch turned onto a narrow dirt road that led to a wooded area where a high bank overlooked the river.

"This is it," Butch said. "Let's get a fire started."

A fire would give us light to see and provide comforting warmth. More importantly, we needed the fire for cooking.

"I'll get some firewood," I said, and followed my flashlight beam along a path paralleling the river. Wood was abundant here, making this a favorite place for nighttime fishing. Butch unloaded the car, setting the food and fry pan next to a bare spot where fires had burned many times before.

The moon provided plenty of light for us to see as our eyes grew accustomed to the darkness. The air was cool enough that mosquitoes were no problem. Within a few minutes, we had a roaring fire that provided enough light for me to see to put a large nightcrawler on my hook and cast it into the water.

The flow of the river was visible under the starry sky, and I felt the rhythmic tug of the current as I propped my rod up with some rocks. I watched the rod tip against the sky, pulsing gently down and up again. Then I settled back against a log and waited, watching for the telltale jerk and bend in the rod that told me a fish was on.

Butch was using two fishing rods, one rigged with a gob of worms and a heavy sinker, the other with a doughball. Doughballs were for carp. My rod was an old casting rod made of steel, a far cry from the light fiberglass or graphite rods available today. We didn't catch carp to eat, just for the joy we got out of catching them.

"Donny! You got a bite," Butch yelled.

Looking, I saw my rod was throbbing. I grabbed it and set the hook. The weight of the fish was immediately apparent. It was a big one. I hauled back and pulled the fish toward me, cranked up slack line and hauled again. This was repeated with first me, then the fish gaining line, until finally the fish was close to shore, and I could make out its swirling in the black water.

"A carp!" Butch exclaimed.

I knew that. But, how to land it on the steep bank was my question. The fish answered it for me. My line tangled in some unseen roots or branches, and my hook pulled loose. The fish was gone.

"Whoa!" Butch said. "That was a nice one. Too bad he got off." But I didn't mind. He had been fun fighting. I baited my hook and cast it out again.

The fire had burned down by then, leaving a glowing bed of embers. And as I propped my rod against the rocks, Butch said, "You gettin' hungry?"

"Sure am."

"Let's get cookin' then."

Butch pulled the fry pan from the sack and laid it across the coals. As he took other things from the sack, he handed me the egg and milk mixture, telling me to shake it good.

Then he placed what must have been a pound of bacon in the pan, not separating the slices. It sizzled when it hit the pan. The smell of wood smoke and bacon soon filled the air. I took a fork and began separating the slices, turning them as they browned, while Butch poured the egg mixture into a metal pot and opened a large loaf of bread, one of two he had brought.

Soon the bacon was done, and we poured most of the hot bacon fat into a can. Butch then dipped slices of bread into the egg mixture and placed them in the hot pan. I had eaten French toast many times, but at home we always had it with sugar and cinnamon. I had never had it with maple syrup before. I did that day. French toast never tasted better. We ate all we could make, two full loaves of bread, and would have eaten more if we had it.

The sky was growing lighter. Clouds hung in crimson layers near the horizon. The gray dawn was showing signs of color as trees stood silhouetted against the sky, and we sat on the log and talked, watching our fishing rods throb with the current.

We caught a few more fish, but by noon, we had had enough. We were getting tired and hungry again. It was time to go. Packing up our gear we headed home in Butch's Chevy, ready for another night and another adventure camping out.

Chapter 20
Wrestling

*W*restling *has always been popular. When I was growing up, wrestlers traveled the country, staging matches at schools and county fairs, taking on all comers. Drawing big crowds, they taunted young toughs who dared not turn down a challenge. Goaded by prize money and the fear of ridicule, one after another, these young men stepped into the ring and were thrown out again.*

While not old enough to wrestle at county fairs, still I was a pretty good wrestler... or thought I was.

Art and I circled each other, each in turn reaching for, then jumping back from the other. I had shed my shirt to show my bulging biceps, rolled my shoulders and flexed my muscles, scowling in my best imitation of Dr. Death.

Foolishly, I had challenged Art to wrestle. He outweighed me by thirty pounds. But his sister was cute, and I sought to impress her.

So here we were, circling, groping, each waiting for the other to be first to let down his guard. I didn't want Art to take me down, for surely, he'd tie me into knots. Then how impressed would his sister be?

From the corner of my eye, I saw her standing just a few feet away, watching us. Again, I shrugged and rolled my shoulders, puffed out my chest and flexed. She had to be impressed, I thought, because she was smiling.

Years earlier, I had tangled with a young man twice my size, and I showed him I was a force to be reckoned with. John and Butch had been standing on the corner near my home talking when I saw them and went over to join in their conversation.

I was a skinny twelve-year old while John and Butch were each fourteen. They were talking about things teenage boys talk about and had no time for a little kid like me. When I came up to them, John told me to go away.

"I don't want to go away," I said.

"Do it anyway."

"Nope."

John tried to push me away, but I grabbed his arm. With his other hand he pushed my head down, so I grabbed his leg with my other hand and held on. When he tried to pull me from his leg, I wrapped my legs around his and latched on to his free arm. Now he was trapped. He was bent over with me anchored to his legs, gripping his arms in both of mine.

Butch stood laughing as John staggered, hardly able to stay on his feet while I clung like a tenacious octopus. Repeatedly, John tried to pry my hands away, but I grabbed at any part of him I could reach. He spun around, reeling, trying to gain control, then finally gave up, saying "Butch, help me! This little brat is like a monkey. I can't get rid of him."

"Sticky little bugger, ain't he," Butch said.

Then John broke into a laugh, realizing the ludicrous situation he was in. Relenting, he said, "OK. You win. You can hang out with us."

Wrestling was popular on television then, just as it is today, although it was not so glaringly phony. We watched Dusty Rhodes, Andre the Giant, Gorgeous George and Mr. Moto. And sometimes we were treated to midget wrestlers like Little Beaver or women wrestlers Cora Combs or Chita Rivera. We enjoyed watching little old ladies pace up and down the ring, shaking their canes and swearing, adding to the spectacle.

Ma Hall was a wrestling fan too. Television was new then, and as radio had been, it provided a gathering place for family and friends.

I often went over to Ma Hall's to watch the snowy black and white images on television, amazed and amused by how she worked herself into a frenzy, screaming at wrestlers and referees alike. "Hit him! Hit him!" she would cry. "Look out for the chair, you Dummkopf!" I had as much fun watching her as the wrestlers.

I once made the mistake of challenging brothers Wayne and Bob to a wrestling match. "I can whip you both at the same time" I said. They looked at each other, grinned, then they jumped on me.

I was older than they were, and bigger than either, but clearly, I wasn't very smart. In a moment, they had me on the ground, with one sitting on my chest and the other across my legs.

Now here I am wrestling Art. Like John, Art was bigger than me and we continued to circle each another while I swelled like a Mississippi boatman "roarin'" about being the offspring of an alligator and descendant of thunder. Still his sister grinned.

Art said, "C'mon. Wrestle if you're gonna."

"I'm waiting for you to make a move."

"Me make a move? You make a move."

"I'll make my move when I'm ready," I said, and we continued to circle.

"Well. Are you ready?"

"I'm getting' ready," I said, continuing to circle Art while swelling my chest, trying my best to look tough.

A couple minutes longer and Art said, "Crimeney. Is this gonna take all day?"

"S'matter? Scared?" I said.

"Scared? Bored. I'd have more fun playing with dolls."

"Like to play with dolls, do you?"

"Nuts" Art said, "I quit," and he turned and walked away.

"Ha!" I said. I won! I knew I could wait you out. That was my strategy, and you fell for it."

With that, Art's sister burst out laughing as she too turned away. Clearly, she was impressed with my humiliation of her brother.

Chapter 21
A Ride to the Beach

Having no organized sports, we had to create our own activities, and swimming was a favorite. But, since waterparks and fancy swimming pools didn't exist, many young people swam in the river or in abandoned quarries. We were lucky in our community. The city had converted an old gravel pit into a sandy beach. Whenever we wanted, we rode our bicycles to the beach where we met friends... and others

We occasionally swam in the river or in a pond at the gravel pit. And sometimes we splashed in one of the wading pools at Riverside or Palmer parks. But this day we were headed for the beach.

Lions Beach was our favorite. Donated to the city by the Lions Club in 1939, it was a gravel quarry in an earlier life. There was a high gravel hill on the backside, but the rest was low and level. A tangled growth of trees and shrubs surrounded much of the area, but the developed portion of the beach was fine sand.

Mike and I rolled our trunks inside our bath towels, jammed the rolls into our bicycle frames and rode off. The beach was two miles away, which was nothing for two boys intent on a day of pleasure away from home. We pedaled along Milton Avenue to Mount Zion, turned onto Ringold and zigzagging up and down driveways. Pedaling rapidly, we leaped our bikes over curbs to make our ride a little more adventurous.

When we reached Tyler Street we coasted down the long hill, at the bottom of which was the Arbuthnot Dairy. We always made it a point to stop there for an ice cream cone on our ride home from swimming. Arbuthnot's ice cream always tasted so much better than any other, before or since. I don't know if that is because it was actually that good, or if the hot day and swimming just made it seem better. Either way, a stop there was a treat we looked forward to with great anticipation.

Soon we arrived at the beach-house; a limestone building one side of which was a changing room and showers for women, the other side for men. An area for beach personnel and clothes storage separated the two.

The bathhouse had tile walls, concrete floors with drains, and no ceiling. It was open to the sky. Wooden benches fronted the changing stalls, and there was an odor faintly reminiscent of bleach. A large, red rubber hose lay coiled near the entry for swimmers to rinse sand from their feet as they entered.

Mike and I left our bikes at the bike rack and hurried inside to change. Some boys were there, changed into their swimsuits already, talking loud and boisterously.

"Hey squirt!" one said to Mike. "Momma bring you down here, did she?" His friends laughed.

"No," said Mike, matter-of-factly. "We rode our bikes. Your Momma bring you?"

"Hey! Don't get smart with me, boy. I might have to straighten you out," he said, pushing his way by as he and his pals sauntered out to the beach.

"Friend of yours?" I asked.

"Just a jerk from school," Mike answered.

Most people placed their clothes in wire-mesh baskets that were entrusted to the care of beach personnel. But since we had nothing of value, we simply changed into our suits and walked quickly across the sand, hot from the summer sun. We left our clothes and towels at a vacant place on the crowded beach and ran to the cooling water.

I never feared the water as some people. I taught myself to swim when I was very young. My parents had brought me to the beach then where I lay on my belly in shallow water, pretending to be an alligator, propelling myself with my hands across the bottom. In that way, I soon found myself in water deep enough where my hands no longer touched, yet shallow enough that I could stand up if I wanted. Before long, my crawling turned into dog paddling and from there into a natural breaststroke.

Mike and I liked to swim to the diving raft in the deeper water, but to do so we had to demonstrate our swimming proficiency to a lifeguard. We didn't mind that. Most of the lifeguards were college students, lean, tan, and female. They wore bright orange swimsuits that distinguished them from other bathers. Two-piece suits were not allowed. We sought out the prettiest lifeguard and showed her how well we could swim, and within minutes were on our way to the diving raft.

At the raft, the lifeguard was perched high above the swimmers on a platform. She wore dark sunglasses and a broad-brimmed hat, and she had a thick mass of white sunscreen on her nose. The loud tough was there with his friends too.

"Whoa!" he said when he saw us. "Look who's here, Tubby and his skinny pal. How'd you get here, Tubby? Rowboat?"

We ignored the loudmouth and hurried up the ladder to the high diving board where I leaped off. Mike followed close behind with a splashing cannonball.

We laughed and challenged each other, duplicating each other's stunts, diving, jumping and splashing. A favorite activity for us was to see who could dive the deepest, reaching bottom and bringing up a handful of sand for evidence.

This soon became too tame as we could do it easily, so we changed our sport to seeing who could stay underwater the longest. To do this, we dove from the side of the raft and swam underwater toward shore.

This turned out to be a better challenge than diving deep, for it was easier to judge the winner, and we didn't have to fear another diver coming down upon us from the raft. Before summer's end we were able to hold our breath long enough to swim from the raft to within wading depth of shore.

A whistle blew at 3 o'clock. Everybody had to leave the water for a fifteen-minute rest period. We used this time to rest, meet other friends, and bury each other in the sand.

Digging trenches with our hands, we took turns getting buried, all but our faces. Then we lay with our backs to the cool, damp sand while the sand above us warmed and dried, forming a crusty coating. It felt soothing to lie there as if in a cocoon, while all around us were the sounds of people playing and having fun.

Suddenly, a boy ran across the sand stepping on Mike as he lay covered. The boy laughed as he ran away, the one we had bumped into earlier.

The whistle blew again, and the rest period was over. As one, the many bathers ran for the water, screaming and yelling, splashing each other. We rose from the sand too, and splashed a bit, washing the sand from our bodies, knowing it was nearly time to head for home. We wanted to leave in time to get an ice cream cone at the dairy, so we headed for the bathhouse.

Inside, we showered quickly and began dressing. Then came the voice of the bully. "Hey Tubby," he said. "C'mere." His friends stood back to watch the fun.

Mike continued buttoning his shirt. "I said come here!" growled the tough as he walked up to Mike, grabbing and lifting him by his shirt.

"Leave him alone!" I said. "He ain't botherin' you."

"Oh? And who are you?" he said, letting go of Mike and coming over to me.

He grabbed my shirt then, stared me in the face and spit, "Whatsit to ya?"

"He's my friend," I said, and I reached my hands between his and took hold of his shirtfront. Lifting upward, I said, "Why don't you pick on someone your own size?"

His expression changed as he stammered, "Put me down!" He had risen up onto his tiptoes as though I was lifting him, but I was no bigger than he was, nor was I a tough looking kid. But clearly, something new was happening to him, to both of us.

He wasn't sure how to react. I wasn't either, but I was filled with delight at his reaction, so I simply told him to get out here and leave us alone, and I released his shirt with a shove. All this while his pals stood in the background, watching. They never lifted a finger to help their "leader." For this, I was glad, because it would never have occurred to me not to help my friend.

Mike and I finished dressing without further incident. After rolling our wet swimming suits in our towels, we hopped on our bikes and rode away, glad for friendships and ice cream.

Chapter 22
Vacation

*S*ome tales tell a moral. Some paint a picture or jog a memory. Still *other stories are a journey in themselves. I hope this story is all of these things as we vacation in northern Wisconsin.*

My thoughts were on spawning bluegills. I pictured myself casting a wriggling worm and watching it squirm as it slowly sank to the nest of a hungry fish. I'd see the fish rush the worm and pick it up and feel the tension on the line. Then I'd set the hook.

With thoughts such as these, I cleaned my tackle and rigged my fishing rods in anticipation of summer vacation. For the last two weeks, I had been watering the garden in the afternoon, and then going out late at night to pick nightcrawlers. I had over ten dozen stored away in a wooden box in a cool corner of our backyard. I was ready.

Every summer my family vacationed near the village of Birchwood in northern Wisconsin. My folks originally came from that area and that was where we were going this time. A long six-hour drive, we were on our way before daylight.

When I was young, I liked to ride in the rear window shelf of Dad's Kaiser Automobile. If that became too warm, I laid on the floor where I put my head against the floorboard and listened to the hum of tires against the road. I was a good rider, but not immune to the question, "Are we there yet?"

To pass time, we made a contest of counting out-of-state license plates, or looked for Burma-Shave signs. Burma-Shave was a popular shaving cream advertised by displaying small signs along the edge of highways in groups of five that might say something like:

"They missed the turn"

"Car went whizzen'"

"Fault was her'n"

"Funeral his'n"

"Burma Shave"

And then there was,

"In this world"

"Of toil and sin"

"Your head goes bald"

"But not your chin"

"Burma Shave"

Another way for us to pass time was by searching for landmarks. The first major one was the Badger Ammunition plant near Baraboo, followed by "The Big Hill." Then came the "river ditches" near Black River Falls where water-filled ditches lined the highway as it passed through a tamarack swamp.

Reaching Augusta, we turned onto highway 27, a highway that led straight north. At Ladysmith I knew we were near our destination. The vegetation looked more like "up north." We had left the oak forests of central Wisconsin and were now among pine and aspen and birch. Even the air smelled different here.

Then Karen said, "There's the 'gooseneck' tree." Looking through the windshield, I saw our landmark, a massive pine tree at the edge of the highway with weathered branches that gave it a shape reminding us of a giant goose.

Just beyond this tree we turned left passing Windfall Lake as we neared Exeland. My cousins Peggy and Sammy lived nearby. Their father, my Uncle Freeman had a farm deep in the woods of Meteor Hills, always a favorite place for me, though we wouldn't be stopping today. We still had to reach Birchwood, but we would return later in the week.

My mother had grown up in Birchwood and many of her family still lived there. My father was from Couderay, a tiny village twenty miles from Birchwood where his father operated a tavern and bait business.

Our destination was Uncle Lester's resort on Birch Lake. Uncle Les was one of Mom's six brothers. I looked forward to our visits each year when I could fish and swim and play with my cousins Judy and Larry. I ran free at home, but here I knew no bounds at all. I got up when I wanted, went where I wanted, stayed out as late as I wanted, did anything I wanted – within reason.

Uncle Les and Aunt Bert had several children, but my cousin Judy was the same age as I, and a Tomboy to boot. She loved fishing and boating as much as I did, so I planned to spend most of my time with her.

Arriving in Birchwood, our first stop was at Grandma and Grandpa Walhovd's. Their white two-story frame home stood on a gently sloping hill near the edge of town. Grandpa had rigged a water pump near the front door with an electric motor so he could pump water with the flip of a switch. Grandma and Grandpa were the first in Birchwood to have such a convenience, all others having to pump water by hand.

Grandpa was a carpenter who had built their home before my mother was born, and many others in the area as well, mostly log buildings. Years earlier he built a greenhouse for Grandma, and as we pulled up, I saw her standing in its doorway with a potted geranium in her hand. Grandpa sat on the porch, smoking his pipe. He waved but didn't get up while Grandma came to greet us as we piled out of the car.

Dad complained of being stiff from the long ride, but I was eager to run and investigate. So, while the others exchanged hugs, I headed for Grandma's hotbeds to see what she had growing. After peeking at

Grandpa's Model "T" I investigated the backyard, noting that Grandpa had built a large, new "four-holer" outhouse.

I wandered through the garden and back to the greenhouse where I looked into wooden barrels beside the doorway. The water in them was alive with wrigglers, mosquito larvae that wriggled and floated just below the surface of the tea-colored liquid. Grandma kept rainwater in these barrels, adding just a bit of composted cow manure each spring to "bring it to life," she said. This "manure tea" was used on all her flowers and was her secret to growing healthy plants.

Inside the greenhouse were benches filled with flowers and vegetables, each in its own clay pot. I inhaled the odor of flowers and soil and composting plants, sorting each one in my mind. Grandma's green thumb had been passed along to my mother, and years later, to me. I loved the smells of earth and plants, whether in a greenhouse or the woods.

The woods. That was our next destination, Uncle Les' resort amid the woods of northern Wisconsin overlooking the lake. The cabins stood on a hillside above Echo Bay, one of several bays and islands we enjoyed exploring. Penny Island, the largest, was also the closest. Twin Islands and Snake Island were other favorites but were at the far end of the lake.

As we pulled in, Aunt Bertha came to greet us. Uncle Les was down by the lake, sealing a leak in one of his wooden rowboats. Cousins Judy and Larry came running up from the pier and I quickly joined them. Grabbing my fishing rod, I hurried down to the lake with them.

A long pier extended into the bay where dragonflies darted, and water striders skimmed the surface like tiny rowboats. Rafts of lily pads spread across the surface and ancient stumps stood above the water, gray and ghost-like on misty mornings. The stumps were like fish magnets to us, targets for a well-cast bait.

We found fish wherever we cast. Bluegills finned in crystal water, one beneath each lily pad, racing to take our baits. Crappies, bass and bullheads, perch and northern pike, one never knew what would be on the end of the line. It was nothing for us to catch a hundred fish in a short afternoon.

We caught and released many fish, keeping just the biggest, for we knew we had to clean what we caught, and big fish were easier to clean.

We had a system, Judy and I, for cleaning them. One scaled and tossed the fish to the other, who with a quick slice behind the head, then along the belly, gutted it. A couple more cuts and the fins were off, and the fish was tossed into cold water for a final rinse. Once we got our rhythm, we could clean two or three fish a minute, making short work of an otherwise unpleasant task.

For supper that night, Mom fixed fried potatoes and the fish we had caught, and the smells of food were joined with those of the woods and water, the "smell of the north woods." All too soon it was bedtime. We had had a long day. I crawled into bed listening to frogs and tree toads and crickets, and the always-pleasant sound of owls. I drifted off to sleep, listening to the splash of fish feeding, and dreaming of tomorrow.

At dawn I awoke to the smell of the water and the sounds of Mom making breakfast. Judy appeared at the door as I came out. Fishing rod in hand, she said, "Let's try West Bay." West Bay was just around the point from our cottage. Shallow and not over six feet deep, it was stump-filled, and weeds and lily pads were abundant.

We tossed our gear into a rowboat and pushed off. A light fog rose from the still water. The distant shore was only faintly visible. Fish dove from beneath the lilies at our approach. Looking around, I saw many dorsal fins cutting the surface.

Penny Island loomed from the fog as we rowed toward the north shore and the entrance to West Bay. The north shore was a crappie hotspot. Boatloads of people, families like ours, anchored there many evenings with cane poles bristling from their boats like the spines of a porcupine, ready to haul these shiny slab-sided fish from the depths.

Judy and I entered the bay and baited our hooks. Setting our bobbers at two feet, we cast our baits into openings in the weeds and as close to stumps as we could. Immediately we were rewarded with fish. Bluegills by the hundreds occupied these waters and it was nothing for us to hook a large bass or two.

We knew where to go for every kind of fish. Bluegills were everywhere, as were perch. We found bass in the shallow water of the bays where they hunted for food. We caught northern pike while drifting across the mouths of the bays and we found crappies in deep water. Rock bass congregated along rocky points that jutted out into the water and a little deeper on those same rocky ledges we caught walleyes.

On the far side of the north shore, an opening we called the "Narrows" connected Birch Lake with Lake Chetac. Judy and I once rowed into the Narrows and far up into Lake Chetac to fish when we were caught in a sudden storm. Rain fell in sheets and the lake was whipped to froth. Rowing hard against the wind and waves, we tried to get back to Birch Lake and home. Had we been smart, we might have gone to shore to wait out the storm, but it was late, and we were expected to be back by suppertime.

The wind increased and the sky grew menacing as dark clouds rolled across the lake. The wind blew cold as a wall of rain nearly blocked our view of shore. Waves crashed against the bow and lightning flashed all around. Unable to make headway alone, each of us took an oar. We were well matched, Judy and I, for she was as strong as I and had grown up handling a rowboat.

Worried, not so much about the storm as about our parents, we considered waiting out the storm on shore. But thinking our folks would be watching for us or even out looking, we decided to go on. There were no homes or cottages nearby to provide shelter, no phones to call from. Landing only meant making our folks worry that much longer. Besides, they wouldn't know where to look for us. We decided to go on.

After much effort, we finally made our way off Lake Chetac and through The Narrows. Then we came to the open water of Birch Lake. Home and dry clothing lay just beyond. But ahead of us were waves that had grown into rolling whitecaps and a wind that hit us full force. Pulling hard on the oars, we inched our way across the lake.

Once, a large wave hit as I was starting to pull on my oar, causing my oar to slip from the oarlock. I fell hard against the bottom of the boat while Judy's oar bit into the water turning the boat sideways. Waves crashed over the side. By the time we regained control, there were several inches of water in the boat, making rowing still more difficult. But finally, the outline of Penny Island appeared through the curtain of rain, and it was only a matter of minutes before we pulled into the protective calm of the bay.

Beaching the boat, we left our gear and ran up the hill to her house. There we found our parents, playing cards, oblivious to our being gone. Mom looked at us standing in the doorway, dripping wet and said, "Where in the world have you two been? You're soaked! You haven't been out in this storm, have you? I thought you two were smarter than that."

The next day, Judy and I were back on the lake this time headed for town. As we neared the mill at the south end of the lake, we passed twin rows of pilings, remnants of a long-gone pier. We rounded the peninsula and entered Little Birch Lake. Ahead were kids swimming and diving at the dam. The dam was a popular place for kids to meet. Some came to meet friends, some to swim. Sometimes we came just to walk in the Red Cedar River below the dam, to tip over rocks searching for mud puppies and hellgrammites.

Mud puppies are aquatic salamanders with external gills and dark spots, with smooth, slick skin. Their tails are flat, and they eat worms and insects found beneath rocks in rivers and streams. Odd-looking creatures, still they are strangely beautiful in their own way, unlike hellgrammites.

Hellgrammites are ugly. Also found under rocks, these larvae of the dobsonfly are cannibalistic and such a fierce predator that they often catch and eat small minnows. We often hunted them for bait when we wanted to fish for perch.

We wouldn't be looking for mud puppies or hellgrammites this day though, because some older boys had removed several of the wooden beams from the dam and water was rushing over with great force, raising the river and beginning to lower the lake.

Resort owners were always concerned when the water level dropped, and it wouldn't take them long to notice and call the town constable to investigate. Judy and I decided not to stay, lest we be blamed or made to tell who had tampered with the dam.

Returning to the resort, my folks were preparing to visit Grandpa Charlie in Couderay, twenty miles away. Grandpa Charlie was my dad's father. Eager to go along, I hopped into the car with them.

Our drive took us through reservation land, home of the Lac Courte Oreilles Indians. We passed Summit Lake on the edge of the reserve, then under a tall railroad trestle where it crossed Hauer creek. The Hauer creek area was a wild place of marsh and swamp, with dense thickets of aspen and dogwood.

Crossing the one-lane bridge over the Couderay River, we came to highway 70. Here the highway parallels this beautiful river nearly all the way from Billy Boy Dam to Radisson. But we weren't going that far. Couderay was only another five miles.

Minutes later I spotted Grandpa's tavern with its dark log walls and fieldstone foundation. Grandpa sold gasoline and live bait too, trapping minnows in the Couderay River. He kept them in his garage in large wooden barrels and I loved playing there, dipping a net into each barrel to discover what he had. I found suckers sorted by size, and chubs, shiners, fatheads, darters and others, all sorted by kind and size, lively in the cold, dark waters of Grandpa's garage.

Grandpa Charlie was a crusty old man, rugged as a lumberjack. A whiskey-drinking, cigar-smoking, Indian-cursing individualist, his voice boomed loud and raspy, and he always had a story or joke to tell. I remember hearing him tell of eating at a restaurant where the steak was "as big as a blacksmith's apron – and just as tough!"

As we entered the tavern, Grandpa's voice boomed out a greeting, and Mattie, Grandpa's lady-friend, came from the back room with a smile. My grandparents had separated many years ago though they had never divorced. Grandpa didn't worry care about propriety. Much different from my mother's parents, Grandpa Charlie did pretty much as he wanted.

My folks sat at the bar to visit, Dad having beer and Mom brandy and sweet, while neighbors, hearing Dad was in town, stopped in with loud hellos to get reacquainted.

The barroom was vast, with a horseshoe shaped bar, dark wood and an overhead fan. Sunlight filtered in through smoky windows. At one end of the room stood a great pool table with massive legs and pockets of braided leather. It was the biggest pool table I had ever seen. Its flat green surface was rich against the darkness of the room. I loved hearing the clack of the ivory balls and was especially happy when Dad suggested I play a game or two with him.

The day passed quickly with my folks visiting and drinking, while I shot pool or explored the garage and nearby river. Periodically I returned to the tavern where Dad would buy me an orange soda and a snack and introduce me to his old friends. I liked sitting there eating potato chips while listening to the stories and laughter that surrounded me.

Then, as darkness fell, it was time to leave. Our drive back through the heavily wooded countryside was always pleasant. The sun's rays filtered through trees and the smells of the pine woods filled my imagination with the creatures that might inhabit that wild country. I tried watching for deer on our way back, but soon was fast asleep.

The next day, Judy and I took our fishing rods and crossed the road to Bennett Lake. There was, in one small corner of the lake near the road, a shallow cove filled with sun-bleached logs. Here the water was no more than three feet deep and generally less than two. Turtles and bass were concentrated in this area, turtles sunning atop the logs, bass half-hidden beneath, waiting for schools of minnows to pass nearby.

Springs fed the lake, boiling up through the sandy bottom, keeping the water clear and cool, making this a favorite place not only for the turtles and bass, but for Judy and me as well. These springs kept the lake alive, until a Chicago area man bought the property, bulldozing a hillside into the cove. The resulting silt filled the springs, ruining the lake forever.

Judy and I caught some frogs to use for bait. Hooking them through the lower jaw, we tossed them in front of the biggest bass we could see. I was always fascinated by the feeding action of bass when they heard the splash and turned, sighted their prey, and rushed to engulf the frog before a rival could beat them to it.

Many creatures acted much the same as the bass. Perch and bluegills fed similarly, rushing to feed or going without. We even caught frogs with our tackle, dangling a wriggling worm on a hook in front of one as it sat along the shore. When it leaped at and engulfed the worm, we simply lifted the struggling frog while it attempted to rid itself of the painful hook by pushing with its front feet, its "hands." I was never bothered by the croaking sounds made by the frogs when caught this way until I was older, then I decided I no longer cared to use frogs for bait.

We were lucky to witness these life-and-death struggles firsthand. It taught us a lot about life – and about death. We learned to appreciate the life and beauty around us, and how fragile it was.

Later that morning, as the day grew warmer, we decided to go swimming at Bennett Lake. A wonderful lake to explore with a pair of goggles, one could swim underwater and view fish close-up through its crystal-clear water and find snails and freshwater clams amid the rocks on bottom. But one didn't swim very long here, for the water was very cold.

In the afternoon I went with my parents to visit Grandma and Grandpa Walhovd, Mom's folks. I hoped we were going to stay for supper. Grandma Walhovd was a wonderful cook and always had fresh bread and pie on the table.

Entering their home, I smelled the yeasty aroma of bread baking. Grandma was in the kitchen, as usual, and Grandpa was in the shed working on something. I heard "Pee Dee," Grandma's parakeet, talking to a mirror in his cage. Pee Dee's cage hung beside Grandma's old upright piano.

Grandma had played piano since she was a young girl, when her mother and father entertained on the old Chautauqua circuit. Before her father's death, her parents performed from Minnesota and Wisconsin, into Illinois. As a girl, Grandma shared the stage with them, reciting spontaneous stories and poems

A round stool at the piano was a favorite of mine. With a dark finish and ornate design like that of the piano, the stool seat screwed up and down with a simple spin. When I was little, I spent many minutes sitting on that stool, spinning around and around.

While my folks visited with Grandma and Grandpa, I visited the attic bedroom where Mom and her siblings had slept. A narrow flight of stairs led to the unfinished attic where, lit by a small window and a single bare light bulb, two vast beds were piled high with homemade quilts. In the middle of the bare wood floor stood a small wood-burning stove that once provided scant heat for the children as they dressed for school.

I had slept here a few times myself when visiting in the winter, sharing something of what my mother had experienced. I especially remembered the weight of the cold quilts and how snug they felt once they finally warmed up. And I remembered waking to see frost riming the roofing nails and rafters, and hurrying, like Mom once did, down the stairway to dress over the heat of the furnace grating in the living room.

At the far end of the room, against the wall, a tall chest held several mementos, most notable of which was a small, beautifully crafted bow and arrows. They stood on an ornate stand with a richly decorated dagger in a scabbard, a souvenir my Uncle Delbert brought home with him from the Second World War. He had said he found it during the fighting and that a Japanese officer had used it for ceremonial hara-kiri.

I thrilled to the treasures that filled this chest, the stories that each one told. This repository of memories probably influenced me to collect and save items useless to others, but precious to me. Things like an old toy, or a snakeskin, or fossils I had found or an arrowhead, things that reminded me of what I truly treasure, experiences and good times.

The smell of dinner reached me about the same time as Mom's voice. "Soup's on. Come down to supper." Meals with Grandma Walhovd were usually meat and potatoes affairs, with fresh baked bread or buns and sometimes pie or cake. The yeasty aroma of her bread, once it reaches your nose, is never forgotten.

After supper, Mom and Dad went downtown to the Bluegill bar to visit old friends, while I went behind the town hall to join the crowd of kids gathering there for the free movie. Every Tuesday night, during the summer, a movie was shown on a white canvas stretched between two poles. This kept the town kids busy and entertained vacationing kids while their parents shopped or visited the taverns.

Judy was there with her younger brother Larry. Judy introduced me to some of her girlfriends who invited me to sit with them on a blanket.

Some people sat in cars, and a few brought chairs, but most just sat on the ground or stood and visited.

There was no end to the activity on a warm summer night in the small village of Birchwood. People were continually coming and going, meeting new friends and old. Laughter floated from the taverns and smells drifted from the restaurants. The mood was easygoing and relaxed.

A group of boys joined us, introducing themselves. They invited me to walk around the village with them, so together we wandered the dark streets of the village, away from the sounds of activity. The boys told me what life was like growing up in Birchwood and asked what living in the city was like, thinking Janesville to be a big city. We shared stories and experiences, and in no time, it was as though we had known each other since birth.

By the time we finished our walk and were returning downtown, the boys had taught me an old song they sang when hiking with the Boy Scouts, *The Ants Go Marching.*

The ants go marching one by one, hurrah, hurrah
The ants go marching one by one, hurrah, hurrah
The ants go marching one by one,
The little one stops to suck his thumb
And they all go marching down to the ground
To get out of the rain, BOOM! BOOM! BOOM!

The ants go marching two by two, then three by three, and so on, until after ten verses, the little one stopped to shout, "THE END!" and we all laughed. Then we began to come upon people walking toward us on their way home, which told us the movie was over and it was time for us to go too.

That next day, my folks planned to visit Uncle Freeman and Aunt Vera on their farm near Exeland. Aunt Vera was my mother's older sister. I was always eager to visit their farm deep in the woods, for it was a primitive adventure for me. Uncle Freeman owned a full section of land, most of it wooded, all of it rocky, from which he and his family eked out an existence.

They lived in a log home alongside the bank of a small stream called Badger Creek. Clear and rocky, I looked forward to hopping across the stream from rock to rock, chasing frogs, watching minnows and water striders, and fishing for small chubs. Occasionally I caught a small trout on hook and line in a dark pool below a culvert where the stream crossed the road.

Aunt Vera greeted us when we arrived. She wore a pair of old-fashioned wire rimmed glasses and had her hair in a bun. From her thin frame, a shapeless dress hung down over her narrow black shoes. My cousin Peggy followed her from the house. Uncle Freeman was away, working in the woods. Their farm was a farm in name only, having just a few cows. Most of their income was from maple syrup and timber.

My aunt and uncle had two children, Sammy and Peggy. Sammy was three years older than I and was a prankster. Peggy was a quiet tomboy. With hair and eyes of deep, rich brown, she was slim but sturdy. Two years younger than I, she was more serious than her brother, yet quick with a smile and ever eager to follow Sammy and me on any adventure.

"Where's Sammy?" I asked.

"Oh, he's somewhere up the hill, I think. I heard him chopping a while ago," Aunt Vera said.

"I know what he's doing," Peggy said. "Come on. I'll show you."

With that, we took off on a run, following the stream uphill. Within a hundred yards, we came to a small pond where Sammy was making a raft about six feet long and four feet wide. He was nailing logs together that were six to eight inches in diameter, securing them with smaller branches nailed to the larger ones.

"What are you going to do with that?" I asked. "You can't go anywhere."

He said, "I just wanted to make a raft to see how well it works. If this works OK, I'm making a bigger one on the Chippewa River and taking it down to the Mississippi."

"You are?"

"You bet. I'm not gonna stick around here all summer," he said. "Wanna help test it out?"

"Sure."

"OK. Hop on then"

Gingerly, I stepped on the edge of the raft, and it began to tip.

"You gotta get in the middle," Sammy said. "You can't stand on the side."

He held it steady while I stepped farther onto the raft. Peggy stepped back.

"Sit down!" he said. "You can't stand on it."

"But it's sinking."

"Oh, it ain't gonna sink."

But it did. Luckily, the pond was only a foot deep along the edge, and even in the middle it wasn't over two. But it was deep enough for me to get my clothes wet.

Returning to the house, we found Uncle Freeman had arrived while we were playing. Mom looked at me in my wet clothes and shook her head. The others grinned, though none so much as Sammy. He delighted in getting me to do anything dumb and I never seemed to fail him.

Uncle Freeman's house was Spartan inside. A hand pump next to the kitchen sink provided water, which then drained back outside again. Aunt Vera cooked on a wood stove, and a round pot-bellied stove filled much of the living area, providing heat in the winter. The wonderful smell of wood smoke permeated their home.

Although they had electric lights and kerosene lamps, their chief source of light came from the windows. And, though small and primitive by many standards, their home was very warm and comfortable.

Uncle Freeman was a quiet man, tall and lean, with a ruddy complexion. He was a man able to work hard and think deeply. Highly regarded by all that knew him, he was a leader in his community, and I enjoyed listening with great interest as he spoke in his gentle tones. With a few words, he was able to express himself with quiet logic on virtually any subject.

My Aunt Vera was similarly intelligent and quiet. And she seemed quite satisfied in living as they did, so far from town and neighbors. I never heard her utter a complaint about working so hard to have so little.

The day was growing late, and Sammy and Uncle Freeman had to milk their few cows, so we bid them goodbye and drove away, promising to stop again before we left for home.

On our return to the cottage, we passed the fire tower that stood high on a hill overlooking thousands of acres of timber on county, state and paper company lands. Each fall, my dad returned here to hunt deer, as would I, eventually. Hunting and fishing were to become an important part of our lives.

It was late when we returned to the cottage. The afternoon was warm and still, the lake glassy smooth. Several boats were out on the lake, filled with fishermen.

Judy was on the pier. I grabbed my fishing rod and hurried to join her. The bluegills were biting as usual, and she had some large perch. I didn't care what we caught. It was all fun for me. But hooking a really jumbo perch was always a special thrill.

In those days, eight and nine inch perch were common. You could dangle a line over the edge of the pier and watch them race for your bait, pulling it away from the smaller ones. But the really big perch were usually caught in the deeper waters of the lake. At night though, even the big fish came into the shallows to feed.

"Don! Supper time," Mom called.

"Got to go." I said. "Meet you here after supper," and I was off.

"Stop gobbling your food" Mom said to me. "You'll have plenty of time to fish. We'll be up at Les and Bert's tonight, playing cards. Don't be out too late."

"I won't," and I was out the door.

Judy was not at the pier when I got there. It was time for her supper by then, so I untied a rowboat, put my tackle and bait in, and slowly rowed out into the weedy bay. Taking my time, I cast my hook with a piece of nightcrawler close to the weathered stumps. The water fairly boiled with life as bluegills and an occasional bass retreated at my approach. But they never went far. There were always more, just below the surface, hidden in weeds, waiting for my bait to land near them.

The sun was hidden behind the wooded hills west of me, glowing against the clouds. A pale blue sky provided a perfect backdrop for the pastel colors glowing from the late spring clouds. A duck quacked softly as she led her brood through a tangle of brush near shore. Frogs croaked. I heard the splash of something, a fish jumping or a turtle sliding off a log, then I heard a door slam, echoing across the lake.

"Don! Come get me," Judy called.

I tugged on the oars and leaned against the weight of the boat, rowing toward shore. The oars squeaked rhythmically as I rowed, water gurgling from the bow. I watched the boat's wake spread in a wide "V" behind the boat and small whirlpools where my oars had cut the water. I listened to the sound of weeds brushing against the bottom of the boat and I sensed the cooling air as evening neared. Someone had a fire onshore – I could smell the smoke.

"Hurry up," Judy called impatiently, waking me from my daydreaming. I turned the boat around and docked against the pier backend first, allowing Judy to easily step into the boat.

"Where ya wanna go," I asked.

"You're doing the rowing," she said. "I'll go where you go."

"Well, let's just work around the edge here and see what we get."

By then, the sun was setting, though it was still light, and the bluegills had slowed their feeding. Bigger fish were beginning to feed and their splashing was heard more frequently as they ambushed their prey. Northern pike were abundant as were bass.

The lake contained large bullheads, and they were now beginning to feed as well. I didn't like cleaning them, but they put up a fight that made catching them a pleasure. We worked our way around the bay, casting into the weeds along shore as the moon rose.

Mosquitoes attacked us if we came too near the shore, so we tried to stay just out of their reach. The colors faded from the sky as a bank of clouds formed in the west. Trees marched in silhouette against the skyline. The air was still.

A loud splash told us bass were feeding in the shallows, and a chorus of frogs surrounded us, croaking, peeping, plunking into the water. Tree frogs, peepers we called them, began their rhythmic songs. Nature was alive all around.

We saw the flickering glow of a campfire onshore and people gathering around, laughing, roasting marshmallows and telling stories. We heard the slam of a screen door. A dog barked.

We had been catching fish, though not very many, nor very fast. But it was a perfect night for relaxing, so we didn't mind. We talked. Judy and I shared what many kids share, about friends, dreaming dreams, hoping hopes, wondering about life.

Though we had grown up many miles apart, in communities that were very different, we had a friendship that was special. We shared things together that we might not talk about with our siblings. Being so close in age and having the same concerns other young teens had, and maybe because we didn't see each other that often, we felt free to talk openly.

A faint flash of light lit up a cloud in the distance. Lightning. The clouds were building in height and density. A slight breeze brought a freshness that told us rain was coming. It was nearly dark, as evening had turned to night.

"Don," a voice floated across the water. "You'd better come off the lake now." It was Mom.

"OK," I answered, and began rowing slowly back toward the pier. Stumps stood like sentinels against the dark waters. Only the gentle squeak of the oars disturbed the sound of the evening.

We reached shore, tied up the boat, and bid each other goodnight. Another day was nearly over.

As I walked down the gravel road to our cottage, I heard the hoot of an owl. It was perched near the cottage, and I fell asleep that night listening to the marvelous sounds of owls and frogs, barely aware of the sound of the rain as it began to fall.

By morning, the rain had stopped. At breakfast, my folks talked about last night's thunder and how it rattled the windows. The storm left behind it a freshness that is hard to describe. The ground was wet, and water still dripped from the trees. Puddles in the road bore witness to the rain, yet I had slept through it all.

That morning we went back to Grandpa Charlie's to visit once more before we would have to leave for home. That afternoon we stopped at Uncle Freeman's again too. The creek was high after the rain, rolling in a torrent down the hill, rather than gurgling and bubbling gently as it usually did.

The smells of the woods after the heavy rain brought to mind mushrooms and moss and earthworms. Birds sang cheerfully. I wasn't so cheerful though, for soon we would be on our way home.

While my folks visited with Uncle Freeman and Aunt Vera, Sammy and Peggy and I walked up the hill through the woods to the upper pasture. From there, one could see many miles, across timbered valleys, until the woods faded into a haze in the distance. In all of that distance, not a building was visible, nor even a sign of man. This was a land I fell in love with; that I would return to every year of my life.

After walking and exploring the woods, we went back to the log farmhouse and sat on the front steps where Sammy, never at a loss for words, talked endlessly. He told about his friends at school, pranks they pulled and stories he had heard, far-fetched tales he swore were true. He said one fellow he knew could tell stories so gory and gruesome that people would throw up just hearing them. And he talked of moving away. Sadly, that was about the only thing he said that seemed believable, he said it so often and with such conviction.

Sammy didn't like the farm. He didn't like being so far from other people. He was gregarious and needed action. Peggy and I just listened. Peggy was always a good listener, very thoughtful, reflective, so when she said anything, I listened. You could believe what she said, for she wasn't one to joke much. Not that she didn't have a good sense of humor, she was just less outgoing about it.

A door slammed. My folks were getting ready to leave. "Don. Come on. It's time to go."

I got up and stepped around the house as my folks were getting into the car. I got in too, looking out the window, seeing Sammy and Peggy standing beside their parents. I didn't realize it then, but within the year, Aunt Vera would be dead, and before too long, Sammy would leave the farm forever, just as he said he would.

Driving away, I took one long last look at Badger Creek, seeing its usually clear, bubbling waters now cloudy, tumbling and boiling against boulders. Nothing stays the same.

We were back at the cottage before dark and, after supper, Uncle Les and Aunt Bert came down to join us in a game of cards. Judy and Larry came along too. Card playing was always popular in our family. Back home, relatives visited nearly every weekend to play, and that tradition continued here.

The next morning was my last day to enjoy the freedom of fishing and swimming and walking in the woods before our long trip back to Janesville. Judy and I took a rowboat from West Bay and, rowing past Penny Island, went around the Point toward East Shore. Following the shoreline, we eventually came to the Twin Islands, near Fernwood Resort.

The Twin Islands rose from the lake's deepest water, nearly sixty feet deep along the north side of the islands. Closer to shore, on the south side, the water was not over twelve feet deep. Patches of weeds grew around the islands, though diminishing quickly on the deeper sides.

Judy and I weren't as interested in fishing as in simply exploring, so we beached the boat on one of the islands and got out. We saw evidence of a campfire in the center of the island. A nice place to sit, I thought, especially at night when one could lay on his back and look up at the sky. We had done that a few times, rowed a boat to the middle of the lake and drifted, watching the stars, and talking. Day or night, the sky seemed huge here in the north.

A smaller island appeared west of the Twin Islands. Barely above water and circled with reeds, Snake Island got its name from the abundance of snakes that inhabited it. This was a favorite place for me to catch northern pike too, in the weeds and reeds surrounding the island. Like snakes, pike seemed ever-present, lying-in wait for their prey.

Rowing the boat past Snake Island, we neared the sawmill and saw steam rising from several stacks and smelled fresh-cut wood. The sawmill provided the principal employment for the town. Timber – its harvest, transport or production – provided jobs and food for most of the local people, along with taverns and the seasonal jobs at resorts.

Continuing our way around the lake, we followed the west shore back toward Penny Island and Echo Bay. Here Birch Lake ran nearly straight as a string with its heavily wooded hillside dropping quickly toward the lake. This was a place where we always caught perch, big perch.

Oftentimes we rowed out to this part of the lake and let the boat drift with our bait inches from the bottom. We caught fish wherever we dropped our lines. Bobberless, we watched the tip of our rods for any telltale tug, and it was here that we found some of our biggest perch.

We alternately rowed, then drifted, fishing from time to time but without enthusiasm. We talked but little as the day wore on, knowing this was the last time we would be together for several months. Soon I would be on my way home. I dreaded the thought.

Finally, it was time to go. Dad had the trunk open, and Mom was packing our clothes. They always packed the car the night before a trip, leaving out only those things we would need in the morning. By first light we would be on our way.

That night I dreamed of the big sky and its millions of stars, of fishing and rowing forever on a lake of glass. I awoke once, late at night, when everything was still but for the chorus of frogs. Then I heard the owl, far away, yet distinct, its call carrying across the waters. Then it was morning.

After a quick breakfast we were on our way. Uncle Les and Aunt Bert were waiting to bid us goodbye, but Judy was not there. Likely she didn't want to say good-bye any more than I did. We had said our goodbyes the day before, on the lake.

We stopped briefly in town to see Grandma and Grandpa Walhovd. Like Aunt Vera, they too would be gone before two more years passed. Waving goodbye, we pulled away. I looked back to see them both, standing, watching, waving until we were out of sight.

We drove east on highway 48, toward Exeland. We wouldn't be stopping to see Uncle Freeman and Aunt Vera this time, and I'd not see Sammy and Peggy or Badger creek again until our next vacation. Nor would I see Grandpa Charlie until then. Vacation was over.

Passing Exeland, we turned south onto highway 27 and passed the gooseneck tree. We went through Ladysmith and then Augusta, and I noticed the vegetation beginning to change already. Asleep by the time we reached the "river ditches," I awoke when someone mentioned "the Big Hill." Baraboo. The Badger Ammunition plant was just below the hill. We were nearly home.

I thought about the fun I had had, fishing, swimming, meeting Judy's friends at the free movie, and walking around Birchwood with the boys I had met, and singing with them, *"The Ants Go Marching."* And I remembered the sounds of the frogs at night and the owls, especially the owls. Their haunting song lives within me yet, reminding me of the north woods.

It was early afternoon when we arrived back home. The first thing I saw was some of my friends carrying baseball bats and gloves. They were headed toward the ball field.

"Hey, Mike," I hollered.

"Hey! C'mon," he said. "We've got a game against the kids from Benton Street."

Dad had hardly stopped the car before I was in the house to get my glove and out the door again. I was home, and my friends were waiting for me.

Chapter 23
Play Ball!

K ids don't know how to play today. Take baseball for instance. Uniformed and fully equipped kids are driven to a groomed baseball park by their mothers where coaches and assistant coaches drill them in all facets of the game. In organized leagues, umpires call balls and strikes, and the score is posted on a scoreboard filled with sponsors' advertisements. Kids use aluminum bats, and families and fans sit cheering in bleachers while eating hotdogs and popcorn hawked from a concession stand manned by other Little League parents.

So, when do the kids get to play ball? I mean really "play" the game of baseball. In play, kids get together to have fun and just coincidentally learn how to get along. Most rules are known ahead of time, but others are created or modified as needed. This is the gist of life, and once it was the gist of play.

In our neighborhood, baseball was played in a vacant lot near Kelly's. Pending ballgames were announced by any boy by simply saying, "Let's have a game after lunch." That's all it took. Every boy in the neighborhood, not off on another adventure, heard about it through the grapevine and appeared in time for the game.

Our ball field was set up on a pie-shaped lot bordered by two converging streets that were crossed by a third. The ball diamond (or more correctly, ball triangle) had no real bases. Instead, our bases were bare spots in the grass. And home plate was not where one might expect it either, with us batting from the point of the triangle to the wider end. Instead, neighborhood tradition placed home plate at the wide end, with Mrs. Kelly's house for our backstop, much to her consternation. Then we batted toward the narrow end of the lot, toward the converging roads.

A well-hit ball might land in the road and roll for extra bases, while a poorly hit one might land in a neighbor's yard or garden, or worse, go through a window.

"No chips on windows!"

That was the cry heard whenever a ball flew toward Mr. Schultz's garage. Not a prayer to the baseball gods but accepted as amnesty from having to share or "chip in" on the cost of replacing broken glass. But you had to say it before hitting the window. Too slow and you shared the expense of restoration.

Rarely did we have the requisite nine players on each team. Sometimes we had only five or six. The two oldest or biggest boys became team "captains" who, once they determined who was to pick first, selected their teams, choosing alternately.

We didn't have regular teams. Anyone who showed up was eligible, and there was no danger of not being picked, only of being picked last. Being the last one chosen was about the worst thing that could happen to a boy. It was bad enough not being a good ballplayer, but having it announced publicly like that was humiliating.

Players came from a wide range of ages so even if you were, say, a poor player of fourteen, you would probably be picked before a ten-year-old who expected to be selected last. But heaven forbid that a "little kid" be picked before you.

When we had fewer than nine players on a team, we played "pitcher's hand is out." That meant, if the pitcher got the ball before the batter reached first base, the batter was out. Another rule served when there were too few fielders. Then the batter had to "pick his field." This meant the ball had to be hit into that field or the batter was "out."

We didn't care so much about keeping score as playing. But, when scores became too lopsided, as they often did, we might choose teams again, or "swap" teammates to balance the sides. Otherwise, the game lost its challenge, and a badly beaten team might threaten to quit.

"Aw, this is no fun. I'm going home."

"Yeah! Me too."

"Wait! We'll trade you Pat for Bob."
"What? Just give us Ron and you keep Pat."
Poor Pat. Being traded like that was sometimes harder than being picked last.

Occasionally, we played with kids from other neighborhoods. When that occurred, scores were important. But innings? We didn't count innings, only who got their "last ups." We might play until dark, then resume the game the next day with the winners being the side who could field a team the longest.

Most of our gloves were old and badly worn, castoffs from older brothers, and not everyone had one. But we usually had enough for the fielders. "I got first dibs on Mike's glove," one would call. With our system of play, the first to "call for" another's glove could use it when he was in the field. Sometimes it was better not to own a glove because you might get "first dibs" on a better one than you could afford.

We didn't have many good bats either, most were cracked and taped. Likewise, while we usually started the season with one or two good balls, soon they had torn covers. When a cover came loose during a game, we simply pulled it off and played on. Balls weren't thrown away simply because they were dirty. We used a ball until it was used up.

I don't mean to imply that we were poor and didn't have much, though that may be true by today's standards. We had plenty. Enough, anyway. We got by because we had no idea there was any other way. We couldn't complain to our folks that we didn't have a good this or a new that, because it never occurred to us that we might get it. We didn't want for things. We simply wanted to play, and play we did.

We played other baseball-like games when we didn't have enough players for a real game. Games like "First Bound or Fly," "Five Hundred" and "Work-up." For "First Bound or Fly," a batter hit the ball until someone caught it on a fly or caught one that bounced no more than once. The one catching the ball then got to hit until another kid caught the ball on the first bounce or fly. This game made a hustler out of everyone, because everyone wanted to be batter. "First Bound or Fly" helped boys quickly gain fielding skills and, as their skills developed, this rapid turnover in batters paved way for the game, "Five Hundred."

In "Five Hundred," one boy batted balls to fielders who earned points based on how they caught the ball. A ball caught on the fly with one hand was worth two hundred points. With two hands, it was worth one hundred points. On the first bounce, it was worth seventy-five, second bounce fifty and after that, twenty-five as long as it was still moving.

Of course, while encouraging competitiveness, this didn't always help the ones who were least skilled, because it was the more experienced who caught and consequently batted most of the balls. But it was fun and taught us to play together.

In playing "Work-up," three boys batted while the others took various positions in the field. The batters then tried to get a hit, and as long as they did, they continued to bat and run the bases. But once they were "out," they had to go into left-field, with the other players shifting to the right, then to third, second, first base, and finally to pitcher. This was a great game and taught us how to play each position.

Then came the Little League ballpark. Little League was new then and its organizers acquired a piece of property on the south side of our neighborhood. They graded and seeded, then built a fence around the field, developing it into a first-class ball diamond. This was something new to us, a regulation ballpark. It was built for the kids in Little League, not for us, but we used it anyway, whenever we could.

When no games or practice was scheduled for Little Leaguers, we moved our ball playing to their new ballpark. Here we found measured base paths and a real pitcher's mound. There were dugouts, a backstop, and a fence that circled the entire field. Bleachers loomed behind the backstop for fans to watch from and in the outfield, a scoreboard complete with advertising. Never before had we known such luxury.

The rules that applied for "sandlot" games still applied here though, except we no longer had to worry about "No chips on windows!" Here there were no windows within range.

The Little Leaguers used padded bases and a thick, rubber home plate, all of which were put away after their games. No matter to us. We could see where the bases should be and simply placed a board or piece of cardboard in its stead.

With a real ballpark to play in, we rarely had to "pick your field" anymore either, because more kids wanted to play baseball. In addition, with kids from other neighborhoods showing up regularly to play, we only had to come up with a single team. So, instead of having two teams, each short some players, we now had extras, and some kids might not be picked before we had a full team. Now play became more serious and scores took on more importance. Now it was our neighborhood against another, and pride became a growing factor.

One day while riding my bicycle through the ballpark, I stopped to watch some of the smaller kids from our neighborhood playing. As I watched, a boy from another neighborhood tried to bully the smaller kids, into leaving the ballpark. He wanted the diamond for his friends who planned to play later in the day. We had always used the "first dibs" rule, that is, those in possession retained possession until they were through. This was true whether at a fishing hole, a parade viewing site, or at a ballpark. The first one there held "squatter's rights."

The boy continued to harass the smaller kids, and then he started getting rough with them. That was when I yelled, "Hey! Leave them alone! They were here first."

He looked at me and said, "Eat rocks, kid. This ain't none of your business."

"Well, I'll make it mine," I said, and started walking toward him.

With that, he pushed a smaller boy out of his way and faced me. Now, I wasn't looking for a fight, but I had opened my mouth in front of all the other kids, so I couldn't back down now. We stood facing each other, just out of punching range, glaring at each other. Then he said, "You wanna fight about it, huh?"

"I'll do what I have to. Those kids were here first."

"So what? I'm here now."

Not willing to throw the first punch, I just stared at him and waited for him to do something. He snarled, "What do you care about these kids for anyway?"

"They're friends of mine," I said, "and they want to play ball. And they're going to."

"That so?"

"Yeah, that's so."

"We'll see about that," he said, and I doubled up my fists, waiting for him to swing. We both circled and glared, staying just out of range of the other.

The other kids started milling about. At first, they cheered, now they were getting bored. First there was no game. Now there was no fight. They wanted some action, but I was in no hurry to give it to them.

About the time I thought they were going to go off and play something else, leaving me to defend an empty ballpark, the bully said, "Well, if you're gonna fight, fight. I ain't got all day."

I just stared at him. Finally, he gave up, saying, "Well, if you're not gonna fight, I ain't gonna waste any more time with you. I got better things to do than stand here all day." With that, he stepped back and walked away.

Relieved, I thought, I just won a fight for right without a blow being struck. I was proud of myself for having stood up to a bully and coming out the winner, though not by much. But the bully had hardly disappeared from view when all the little kids disappeared too, headed off in another direction, no longer interested in playing baseball.

Chapter 24
Ghost Stories

Young people today enjoy realistic movies and electronic games with themes designed to scare or shock purely for the thrill of being frightened. We enjoyed being frightened too but found it in other ways. Our movies were black-and-white and not very realistic, yet our imaginations made up for that lack which sometimes made things even more frightening.

Shared experiences have always brought people closer together. In our neighborhood, we shared many things, one of which was Ma Hall's ghost stories. There, in the dark of a summer night, we shared experiences that brought each of us closer.

The news spread through the neighborhood with electrifying speed, "Ma's gonna tell ghost stories tonight."

"What time?"

"Dark."

"I'll be there."

Ma Hall's fame as a teller of ghost stories was well known among us kids. She had a way of telling tales that kept us huddled together for safety. We were enthralled by her tales, afraid to listen, yet afraid to leave. Where she grew up in the hills of Missouri, storytelling was a way of life, an art form and she was a master.

Several times each summer, we kids got together to tell ghost stories, repeating those we had heard. One of us might try to make up a scary story on our own, but almost always they turned out to be more laughable than frightening. We just didn't have what it took, and Ma did.

Ma Hall sat in her lawn chair talking with some of the early arrivals as others continued to come. Some brought blankets and all vied for a place close to Ma. Her son, Bud, looked forward to these nights as much as anyone, because by the end of the evening a girl or two would be so afraid she would need someone to walk her home.

Sometimes we enjoyed the comfort of a small fire built more for ambience than for any need to keep warm. Its eerie glow was an important part of the evening, providing comfort while casting shadows that danced in the dark, lending an evil look to Ma's face.

Ma didn't just start telling her ghost stories immediately. First, she allowed the darkness to deepen while conversation naturally drifted toward things that go bump in the night. That was her secret. That was part of the art of telling ghost stories. One couldn't just *tell* them with any hope of good effect. No. You had to wait until the mood was right naturally. Then the stories became more real. Then it didn't matter if you had heard a story a hundred times before. With the right atmosphere and the right storyteller, the most familiar story takes on new life.

Darkness covered us like a blanket, and our conversations drifted from playing to the first tentative tales told by some of the kids. This often resulted in nervous titters in anticipation of the real thing, or outright guffaws for a missed punchline in a familiar story.

Ma's voice slowly became more prominent as she talked about the day's activities, then of friends and family, and finally to recollections of her youth. With this came the first hints that a story was about to unfold.

Other conversations faded away as we listened to Ma's voice become more descriptive, her inflection adding color. Soon, all conversation ended as we sat enthralled by the visions conjured up by her haunting voice. Her tales turned to unexplained events, appearances or disappearances, then to stories of people missing or found dead.

All around us was quiet as a graveyard as Ma allowed the tension to build, and then subside, only to mount again. Repeatedly, like waves crashing on the shore, our level of expectation swelled and fell, keeping us on the edge of our seats, listening to her every word.

Then, when the moment was ripe, she provided a crashing ending in a sudden blow that nearly swept us from our blankets in screams and nervous laughter. The only thing keeping some of us from running home was the darkness and fear of what might be lurking there.

Many stories Ma told are well known, like *The Hook, Buried Alive,* or my favorite, *The Golden Arm.*

"Many years ago," Ma began, "a young woman lost her arm in an accident. Her father, being very rich, had an artificial arm made for her out of purest gold."

Ma looked around to see that we were all listening, then she went on.

"The young woman grew up and married. But soon she became ill. Realizing she would die soon; she made her husband promise to bury her with her golden arm.

"Her husband promised, and when she died, he buried her as he said he would. But then he thought, 'What have I done? I can get a lot of money for that gold. I could be rich if I sold it. Besides, I did as I said I would. I buried her with it. I didn't say I would keep it buried.'

"So that night he went to his wife's grave, dug up her casket and opened it. There she was, with her golden arm shining in the glow of his lantern. So, he took it from her body and went home."

We kids were growing uneasy by then, looking at one another to see how others were reacting. Nobody wanted others to know they were frightened. Some simply stared straight ahead hanging on Ma's every word.

"That night," Ma said, "as the man was drifting off to sleep, he thought he heard a voice downstairs saying 'Whooo has my gooolden arm?'" and she drew the words out in a ghostly and ghastly manner.

"The man awoke with a start," she said. "But decided he had only imagined it and went back to sleep.

"A while later he heard the sound again, this time on the stairway. 'Whooo has my gooolden arm?' Frightened, he tried to convince himself it was nothing and tried to close his eyes.

"But then he was roused once more by the voice. 'Whooo has my gooolden arm?' This time the voice was just outside his bedroom door. He was really getting scared now and pulled his covers over his head.

"He lay there for several minutes listening, when suddenly he was startled to hear the voice still closer. Peering from his covers he looked and saw the bedroom door was open, and there before him stood the shadowy figure of his dead wife.

"Whooo has my gooolden aaarm?" she said, "Whooo has my gooolden aaarm?"

"YOU DO!" Ma shouted, and everyone jumped in fright.

Evenings like this took place only two or three times each summer, often enough to be popular, yet rare enough to be special. And Ma Hall was like that too, a rare woman who was special to many of us who were lucky enough to grow up in the Boies Addition.

Chapter 25
Adventures

*B*oys thrive on adventure, and one of the best things for a boy growing up in the Boies Addition was the adventure he found at every turn. Of course, one person's adventure is another person's trouble, but however you define it, ours was a glorious childhood.

June bugs thumped against the screen when I heard Mike calling from the street. "Donnn!"

"Be right there," I said as I got up from the table.

"Where are you off to tonight," Mom asked.

"Out," I said, and I dashed out the door to meet my friend.

My parents always had a hard time keeping track of me. I might say I'd be at Mike's," while he told his folks he'd be at Ron's, and Ron would tell his parents he'd be at my house. Even we didn't know where we would be much of the time.

"What's up," I said, "Where d'ya wanna go?"

"I dunno. Just figured we'd walk around and see what everybody is up to.

If it were daytime, we might walk across the fields as we often did, to the city airport to watch the single-engine airplanes take off and land from the grass runway. Or, also at the airport, we might play in the fuselage of the old, wrecked biplane that lay beside one of the hangers.

Some days we went to the river to hang out around the "cave," an underground storage cellar known to few others, the remains of an old brewery. Just getting to it was an adventure to us as it meant crossing the railroad trestle that spanned the river near the Centerway Street Bridge. Here we often bumped into hoboes, men we innocently thought to be poor and simple travelers, though today we know them to be men who are far more dangerous to young boys than we imagined. But fortunately for us, our imaginations told us to give them a wide berth.

Crossing the trestle was more of an adventure for us when we crossed from beneath, balancing on the iron support beams that crisscrossed the structure many feet above the river. One slip meant an eternal end to our adventures, but we never gave it a thought for we were immortal.

But these nighttime adventures were very different from those of the daytime, made more exciting by the darkness. Last week we walked out to the Highway 26 outdoor theater where we sneaked in over the fence. And a few weeks earlier I had joined Bud in his search for a battery for his Henry Jay automobile. We found one in a car sitting in the Desen's Used Car lot.

Lightning bugs by the hundreds rose from the field across the street, circling in slow motion, blinking their coded messages as we walked together. Far to the north, heat lightning flashed against distant clouds near the horizon. I enjoyed the sounds and smells of the humid summer evening, felt the gentle breeze while wispy clouds floated across the moon.

We found ourselves headed toward Dryan's ice cream parlor where some friends had gathered outside. A few days earlier we had stood out front like that, pretending to be beating up our friend, Mike. Pulling our punches, three of us playfully pummeled him, while he clutched his stomach and fell to the ground as though in painful agony. Then we continued as if we were kicking him.

Our playing must have appeared realistic, for suddenly a group of men burst from Slick's tavern and started to cross the highway intent on breaking up our "fight." But they stopped just as suddenly when we, including Mike, the one being "beaten," waved at them with smiles and laughter. Then, with arms around each other's shoulders, we entered Dryan's for a Coke.

"Damn kids!" I heard one of them say while the others mumbled in agreement.

We planned nothing like that tonight though. Instead, we just talked and joked about some of the things we had done recently. Earlier in the month, we had "camped out" together. That didn't mean we slept. Rather, it meant we walked the streets all night long, just talking. We went down the Black Bridge Road where we came to the railroad tracks and followed them into town. In town, we watched the late-night activities of older kids as they drove the "circuit." One day we would be old enough to have our own cars, and we could drive the circuit too, we thought, and maybe pick up some girls.

I had found a ride with an older friend a few days earlier and told my friends about it.

"Terry picked me up and we went toolin' around town the other night where we saw these two girls. We waved at them, and they hopped right into the car.

"This one girl started talking about her dad. Said he was real mean and beat her mother. He worked for the railroad. He was a big guy, and she was scared of him.

"She asked us to drive by her place, near the hospital, so she could get something, so we did. She said to drop her off a block away and she'd walk home, not wanting anybody to see her riding with us. She said to just drive around the block and she'd meet us by the next corner. So, we left her and drove around.

"Her girlfriend stayed in the car with us and told us more. She said the girl was planning to run away, 'cause her dad beat both her and her ma. He was real mean.

"Well, we got to the corner and the girl comes runnin' like crazy. 'Let's get outa here,' she screamed, 'She's dead. She's dead. He killed her,' she kept saying over and over. She said she saw her mom layin' on the floor between the bed and the wall and she was dead. So, we drove off wonderin' what to do. Then Terry and me, we thought we better go back and see what's goin' on for sure.

"We turned down this one street and the girl screamed, 'There he is! That's my dad. Don't let him see me,' she says. Well, we see this big guy walking up the sidewalk, all dirty, ya' know, still a couple blocks from the house.

"Well, Terry, he says we gotta find out. Maybe her mom's just hurt. This girl's panicking by now, but we go back to her house and her girlfriend says she'll go in to see for sure. So, in she goes.

"Well, turns out she wasn't really dead. Dead drunk is what she was. Well, we dropped those girls off downtown and left 'em. Couple of 'Screamin' Meemies' they was."

"Peddidle!" someone shouted and slugged me hard on the shoulder. That was what we did when we saw a peddidle, a car with a headlight out.

George said he wished Terry would come by and pick us up. "Maybe we could go 'sailing.' Sailing is what we called driving fast over the bridge, because that is what the car does. Go too fast and the bumper slammed against the road. Too slow and you hit your head on the roof. Sailing was going just the right speed.

"Hey! Anybody ever been knocked out?" Mike asked.

"Whatcha mean?"

"I mean, 'knocked out, unconscious."

"Yeah, sure."

"No really. It's easy. You just take a bunch of deep breaths and stick your thumb in your mouth. Then you blow hard, and you pass right out."

"Why would ya do that?"

"It's fun. Here, I'll show you how. Pat. Take some breaths, real deep. I'll stand behind you and keep you from falling. After you take about ten or fifteen, I'll squeeze your chest from behind while you blow against your thumb.

"You're sure?"

"Sure, I'm sure. I'm not gonna hurt you."

So, Pat took a bunch of deep breaths and blew, his eyes shut and cheeks puffed out, while Mike reached across his chest and squeezed, lifting him from the ground. In seconds, Pat was limp, and Mike laid him down on the ground.

We stood there amazed as Pat roused a few seconds later. "What happened?"

"You were out Cat Man."

"Yeah, like a light."

"Wow!"

Just that fast we had started a new fad and were dropping like flies just to experience unconsciousness. Fortunately, no one got hurt. Fortunately, too, the fad passed quickly before someone was hurt.

We hung around the ice cream parlor a while longer hoping someone with a car might show up, but no one did, and one by one we drifted away to wait for the adventures of another day.

The next day I ran into Schultzie, and having little else to do, we wandered the neighborhood looking for friends. One of our friends was Kennard, though we called him Kenny... and many other things as well.

Like my brother who teased me, Schultzie and I enjoyed teasing Kenny whenever we had the chance. Kenny was thin and gangly, and we teased him about his awkwardness. We taunted him so much that we drove him into his house. But we didn't let a little thing like a door stop us from continuing. We stood outside throwing jibes at him for several more minutes until he came to the door... carrying a shotgun.

But even the shotgun didn't stop us from continuing our taunts... until he pulled a shotgun shell from his pocket and dropped it into the chamber. That stopped us, but only for a few seconds, for we saw he had inserted a shell that was too small, and it had lodged in the barrel.

That gave us the ammunition we needed to jeer at him even more. "What a dumbbell you are. Can't even load a shotgun without messing it up. Har! Har!"

"Maybe I should get my sister to do it for you. Ha! Ha!"

Kenny was so angry, by now he was shaking. Holding the gun upside down, he shook it, trying to dislodge the shell, threatening and uttering obscenities at us as all the while we rocked on our heels with laughter.

But then he did something that really scared us. He pulled another shell from his pocket and dropped it on top of the first one, and this one fit.

"Kenny. Stop!"

"Yeah. Hold on Kenny. That thing'll blow up if you try to shoot."

"I don't care. I'll blow you up too," he said as he closed the action and raised the gun to it point at us.

"Wait! Wait! Geeze, Kenny, hold on. We were just teasin'. We don't mean nothin' by it."

"Yeah. We didn't mean anything."

By that time, two of Kenny's brothers had come to see what the commotion was all about. They took Kenny's side against us, as they usually did, which helped calm Kenny somewhat. He knew he wasn't going to have to take any more of our ridicule without support from his brothers as they all lined up against Schultzie and me.

"Kenny. You know you're our friend. We were just having fun." And we were, even if it was at his expense.

Kenny began to settle down a little, and finally pointed the gun up. "All right. I'll let you guys go this time. But I want you out of here. And don't come around here anymore. Besides, I wouldn't want to have to clean up the mess if I shot you."

Schultzie and I left, and I began to realize that I wasn't the only one hurt by teasing. Perhaps what we call adventures could get out of hand.

Chapter 26
Our Gang

Gang activity regularly makes news today, and many young people probably think gangs are something new, something of their generation only. But gangs have always been around. They were popularized in the 1950's with the musical "West Side Story." That, I think, is where we got the image of gang members with their hair slicked back, tight fitting jeans and leather jackets.

Gangs have been popular because they give a person a sense of belonging. I was a gang member too, although I didn't exactly present myself in the image of Tony in "West Side Story."

I hounded my mother to let me get a leather jacket, "like all the other kids." "You're not all the other kids," she informed me. "Besides, we just bought you a new coat last year."

"But Ma," I protested, "I look like such a nerd. Besides, that coat doesn't fit any more."

Truth was, my coat was made of cloth, had button-down flaps over the pockets and a buckle in front. It just didn't communicate the image I wanted. Anyone seeing "West Side Story" knows what I mean. A black leather flight jacket with zippers on each of its many pockets and a collar you could put up was essential. Everybody knew that.

No boy would be accepted as a mature, independent man until he dressed the part. So, I whined and begged until Mom finally relented and I got my way – sort of. Except what I got, wasn't a tight-waisted leather jacket but a three-quarter length vinyl plastic coat. And it wasn't black but off-white. And the only zipper it had was the one up the front. And as for a collar... well, it was cloth and nothing I could turn up.

"But Ma!"

"Don't 'But Ma' me. This is what you get. Take it or leave it."

I took it.

To complete the image, one had to have hair combed back on the sides and a large "wave" in front, Elvis Presley-style. But Mom was the one who cut my hair and she gave me two choices, parted on the side in what I would call a "choir boy" style, or a "flat-top." I opted for the flat-top, simply because, as it grew longer, I could comb the sides back and the top forward with a part in the middle ending in something like a "spit-curl" rather than a "wave." Blue jeans and metal cleats on our shoes completed our uniform.

Our "gang" was nothing organized with a leader or anything, and not all of its members thought of themselves as in a gang. In fact, few probably ever thought that. What we called "our gang" was nothing more-or-less than all the kids in our neighborhood.

Every neighborhood had a gang, usually like ours, just a natural grouping of kids seeking their niche in the social order. Each group felt they owned certain turf, their neighborhood, and they wanted others to know it.

Neighborhood rivalries were natural. This was as true then as it is today, just like the rivalries between cities or schools. But, unlike today, there were seldom any real power struggles between groups.

Oh, a few of us sometimes carried knives and even chains, but not with any intention of getting into fights or anything. It just seemed the thing to do; the role we were expected to play. And, though Schultzie and I experimented by making ""zip-guns," we never carried them anywhere.

Looking back, it's easy to see how kids today might get into trouble without ever having intended to. We were very lucky.

A favorite activity on Friday nights were "jam sessions" held at the old Armory building downtown. There, live bands played rock and roll music and we had a great time meeting kids from school and making new friends. And seldom were there any fights.

Seldom, that is, but for one night after a jam session when we were walking home. We had just passed the Jeffris theater when we heard the screech of brakes. A car stopped quickly, trapping another car between a third. Two boys jumped from the lead car, boys who, oddly enough, in later years became community leaders.

They ran to the middle car, jerking the back doors open as we stood there, astounded to see, first a shoe, then part of some clothing fly from the car as the two beat another young man severely. By the time the driver of the third car realized what was happening and backed away to let the center car out, the attackers ran back to their car and sped off.

Usually, we enjoyed wandering the streets downtown for hours, but not that night.

Some nights later we decided to go to church. Not that any of us were particularly religious at the time, but we had heard rumors about a church in our neighborhood and wanted to learn if the stories we heard were true. The stories told of people in trances shouting and writhing on the floor and in the aisles, and oftentimes we had heard shouting, singing, and music that grew louder and livelier the longer they went.

The church members all wore simple clothing, and the women wore no makeup or jewelry. For those reasons and because the members of the church were from outside our neighborhood, they were different, and being different meant they were fair game for ridicule.

The young men of the church had often seen us peeking through the windows and hurried out to confront us when they found a break in their service. Nevertheless, we wanted to see for ourselves what they did within that building. We knew if we went inside instead of listening at the windows, they would treat us as guests.

After daring each other to visit the church, the girls decided they would wear makeup and gaudy earrings, while we boys dressed in our best gang clothing, leather jackets and all.

I wore my off-white, plastic-leather jacket, trying to look as "cool" as anybody, though somehow, I don't think I succeeded very well.

Meeting at the vacant pump-lot, we walked to the church where several of the young men sat on the front steps. They were ready for us. But, before anything happened between us, their minister came out. Realizing we wanted to come in, he cheerfully invited us to sit right up front, but we declined, filling instead the pews in the back.

We were not disappointed. The sermon was lively and the music loud. They knew we were not there out of any greater desire, yet the adults treated us pleasantly, though the stares from the young men were hostile.

Midway through the evening, they took what amounted to an intermission, providing us an opportunity to leave. Again, we passed through the gauntlet of young men standing outside the front door. Certainly, we tried their faith that night.

Our appetite to investigate was satisfied and we never bothered them or looked in through their windows again.

Later that summer, seven or eight of our gang, both boys and girls, went bowling. It was late and the bowling alley was nearly deserted. Another group of boys from high school was there who kept looking at us. Having seen some of them before, I knew they could be trouble.

In time, I had to go to the bathroom, having to pass through the men's locker room. On my return, several from the other group were waiting for me. Surrounding me in the locker-room, they pushed me around, alternately holding, slapping and threatening me for several minutes.

My friends soon became aware of the situation, and I saw them standing outside the locker-room door. I expected them to come to my aid, but they just looked on uneasily, making no effort on my behalf. I was confused by their inaction.

Then they disappeared. I thought they were going for help, at least I hoped they were. Meanwhile, the toughs continued their onslaught until, tired of their game, they shoved me out the door.

Disheveled but not injured, I looked for my friends, and finally found them standing by their car in the parking lot. Seemingly concerned, they asked if I was all right, but never did they attempt to help. This opened my eyes to the limitation of friendships.

Chapter 27
The Knife

While going through an old desk, I spotted a jackknife I've had since I was a boy. With two blades, each about 3" long, it shows evidence of much wear from repeated honing. The brown handle is bone-like and has a chip out of one side. The other side has a small plate with the word "Sabre".

The knife was given to me by a boyhood friend when I was twelve and reminds me of those days of friendship and freedom, and George, the boy who gave it to me.

A boy just isn't complete until he has his very own jackknife. Very lucky boys have one given to them by their fathers. But boys of ordinary luck had to buy their own. I was happy enough to have ordinary luck.

My friends and I took pride in keeping our jackknives carefully honed, vying for the honor of having the sharpest knife. Consequently, my knife-blade was thoroughly worn down from constant sharpening, its point being almost needle-like.

I was not a newcomer to knives. I had experience. My mother once gave me a paring knife and a block of balsawood, suggesting I try carving something. She did this, no doubt thinking it would occupy me for a few days and keep me out of trouble. But, of course, it did no such thing.

I chose a modest project to begin with. A simple duck decoy. Then, while holding the block of wood between my knees, I began whittling, slicing slivers of wood from the block. About ten minutes into my carving, my knife slipped and cut a neat chunk out of my leg just above the knee.

I remember staring at the wound through my cut pants, seeing pale white fat below. Then, as I watched, specks of blood appeared, slowly at first, and then running in torrents.

A quick ride to the doctor and a few stitches put everything right again, though Mom surely questioned her wisdom in giving me that project.

I also had experience in the use of corn-knives, having once been hired by a local farmer to cut thistles from his hay field. At first, I imagined the corn-knife as a machete and I an explorer, slashing my way through a vast jungle. But the novelty of swinging that machete quickly wore off in the summer sun.

While I quickly lost my enthusiasm for swinging a large corn-knife, I never lost my love for my jackknife. Just knowing one is in your pocket makes a boy feel more like a man. A boy with a jackknife felt he was able to meet any challenge, and one of the challenges we faced was a game of "splits."

To play splits, two boys stood face-to-face and toe-to-toe, then threw their knives out to the side, trying to stick them into the ground. Our rule was they had to be thrown by their blade, so they flipped end-for-end at least once. If your knife stuck, your opponent had to "split" to reach that point with his nearest foot. If he reached it, he then threw his knife and stuck it into the ground, and *you* had to split. This continued until one could no longer split far enough to reach, thus the other was declared the winner.

Boys challenged each other, winners playing winners and losers playing losers, until we were satisfied that one of us was the Champion. After that, we played again until a new Champion was declared or until we tired of the game and went off to play something else.

My friends and I played splits, off and on, through much of the summer. Eventually we became so skilled that we could throw and stick our knives into the ground at ten or twelve feet, well out of reach of our opponent. It got so that the winner was often the first one to throw. Thus, the game lost its challenge and therefore our interest.

But, one day while we were playing, George threw his knife, striking mine, breaking it. Without a moment's hesitation, he gave me his knife in exchange for mine.

Now, breaking a knife in a game such as ours was one of the risks we took. Just as someone's shooter might shatter a marble, I never expected George to give me his knife. But he insisted. That's the way he was. George was a good friend.

Chapter 28
The Devil's Staircase

S *ometimes boys got together to do – well – nothing. Just to be together.* *Sometimes we spent whole days doing just that. Nothing. And, what's* *wrong with that? Nothing.*

After lunch, I rode my bike over to Mike's. Ron was there already.

"What's up guys?" I asked.

Mike said, "We're gonna take a ride to Riverside Park."

"And do what?"

"How 'bout we ride back along the Devil's Staircase?"

"Alright," I said. "Let's go!" and we were off. Ron led the way on his racing bicycle. Mike and I followed, he riding his middleweight bike, I on what was left of my three-speed racer.

We rode south on Milton Avenue, then took Benton following the back streets. Riverside Park lay across the river, on the northwest side of town, about a four-mile ride for us. A popular place for families, Riverside offered picnic tables and shelters, fishing, wading and water from an artesian well.

Cold water with a slightly rotten egg smell flowed from the well, though it came from nearly a thousand feet below the surface. The water was pure and crystal clear, bubbling up a large pipe, spilling into a limestone lined pool. From there, it went into a wading pool where the water warmed slightly in the summer sun.

We three rode side-by-side for a while, then in follow-the-leader fashion as one after the other we rode up and down driveways, leaping over curbs, following sidewalks, wending our way along. Coasting down the Glen Street hill, we soon crossed the river on the Centerway Bridge. A tall railroad trestle loomed above on our right, a place we had often stopped to play, but not today.

We turned onto a footpath along the river that led northward, past a hole in the ground that we sometimes visited, especially on hot summer days. This hole opened up into a large underground room cut from natural limestone many years before when the old Croake Brewery was located here. Long forgotten by most, the entrance was repeatedly filled in by adults who didn't want us there. But we and other kids who knew of this place, found it to be the perfect hideaway, so each time the entrance was filled in, we dug it open again.

But today we rode passed, taking the path as a shortcut, avoiding streets and traffic. Besides, it was more adventurous this way, and we commonly did what we could to avoid civilization, for that was the purpose of most of our adventures.

In a short while we came to an old railroad viaduct. Built of immense limestone blocks in 1925, this marked the entrance to Riverside. Coasting through the archway, we passed the roller-skating rink and rode into the park.

Rays of sunshine filtered through trees that framed the road. We followed the road, coasting along on our bikes parallel to the river. Several families were picnicking near a wading pool and fishermen sat along the riverbank. Some couples sought seclusion, walking hand-in-hand or lying on blankets in the grass.

We rode our bikes past the boat launch where the river widened. Water sparkled in the sun. I saw a carp jump, and an armada of ducks floating near shore. A large hawk sat motionless in a tree watching the activity.

Where the road curved, I looked for the hidden shell of Camp Cheerio in the thick woods across the river where it lay unseen, unknown by most.

Riding further into the park, the trees thinned out, giving way to ball diamonds and open grassy spaces. Tall, spreading willows waved along the edge of the river.

Ahead, I saw another wading pool, this one filled with children, splashing and laughing. Beyond the pool stood a concession stand and a comfort station, each built of the same limestone.

"There it is!" Mike said, pointing. Behind the concession building, we saw a stone stairway that led up a wooded hill. Between that hill and the river was the footpath we sought. Dubbed "The Devil's Staircase" by local tradition, this pathway led one beneath tall trees, through damp vegetation and walls of dripping moss-covered limestone.

Immediately, we headed for the trail. This trail was not intended for bicycles. It was narrow and winding, of hard-packed earth, paved in some places with stone. Yet, we rode up and down the path as the land curved, bouncing and bumping farther into the "Staircase," with the hill on our left and the river immediately to our right.

We met very few people, and we occasionally scattered flocks of ducks that were foraging near the shore. Startled, they took off, scattering and splashing into the river. Bird life was abundant here. I watched the swirling current as the muddy Rock River flowed southward.

We were surrounded by verdant green vegetation. Ferns and moss covered the hillside, water trickled, dripping over rocks, falling from ledges, seeping along the ground. The pathway led us at times across ledges where slabs of rock hung out over the river. We had to walk our bikes up some of the stone steps, while we bounced down others, barely able to control our descent as we rode.

Cries of laughter told us someone was ahead. Then we came to a small ravine near the end of the trail, created over eons from water that flowed toward the river. Left behind were the rocky steps we called the "Devil's Throne" and indeed, it reminded one of the throne of a giant. Secluded as it was, one might easily feel a mysterious foreboding, especially anyone foolish enough to be here after dark.

More laughter rang out and we heard splashing. Some kids were swimming in the river. They had a heavy rope tied high in a tree that leaned out over the water. How anyone had dared to climb so high to fasten it there, I couldn't imagine.

I watched as one boy took the end of the rope and climbed the rocky ledge leading away from the river. Then, holding to it tightly, he leaped from the edge, swinging far out over the river where he let go and fell to the water below.

This had been a popular place for young people to gather whether to swim or just to meet. Boys liked to bring their girlfriends here for its seclusion. Adults enjoyed it simply for the beauty. We enjoyed it for the promise of adventure it and our imaginations provided.

Following the main pathway back, we took short detours, exploring faint trails through the rocky bluffs. By the time the afternoon sky began taking on warm colors, we found ourselves by the wading pool again where we slaked our thirst, drinking deeply from the artesian well. Then we headed home. We had had no particular objective, nothing special to accomplish, nothing other than spending the day with friends and delighting in our freedom. And sometimes that is enough.

Chapter 29
"Wheels"

*M*y grandmother lived to see men land on the moon, and as a girl, she saw covered wagons pass by her home in the hills of Missouri. She never got over how transportation had changed, and the rate of that change.

From the moment I learned to walk, I dreamt of freedom. To a boy, what represents freedom better than his own "set of wheels?"

Transportation was simple when I was a small child. I was carried. That wasn't too bad. It was comfortable and warm. But it was limiting, and I never liked limitations. At first all I could do was go from my crib to a highchair to a stroller where I sat playing with beads and watching Mom do housework. I wanted more than that.

After learning to walk I was given a tricycle. Not a new one, but it was mine and I rode the wheels off it, pedaling all over our neighborhood. Sometimes I placed one foot on the rear axle and pushed myself along with the other foot as one might a scooter. Other times I sat on the rear axle with my feet on the pedals, racing around the yard and the neighborhood with my own version of a "low rider."

Eventually I received a bright, shiny Radio Flyer wagon and I used it much as kids do skateboards today, for transportation. With one knee in my wagon and a hand on the rail, I flipped its handle up and back for steering, and pushed myself around the block with a rattle and a roar. My friends and I raced this way, eventually teaming up with one riding and the other pushing, racing at high speeds – or as fast as our "motor" could run.

We organized wagon races with other kids, running pell-mell down the block and back until our motor tired. Then we traded places and raced some more. All summer, it seemed, we raced. I say, "it seemed," because, when you are a young boy, you can crowd a month's worth of activity into a day.

But I used my wagon for more than racing. I brought pails of water home from the community well, and more than once carted my father home from Slick's tavern in it. My wagon was truly an all-purpose vehicle.

Boys naturally enjoy taking things apart to see how they work, and I admit, there isn't much to a wagon, but that was no reason not to take it apart. I pulled the wheels off at least once a week to grease them, oiling the steering mechanism and tightening every screw and bolt. I took very good care of my wagon.

My next "set of wheels" was a pushcart. Not a fancy, soapbox derby racer, just a couple of two-by-four boards fashioned together in a "T" loosely connected by a single bolt. I mounted a pair of wagon wheels to the long axle at the front of this "T," and a second pair at the rear. That's where I sat, at the rear of the "T" with my feet on the front cross-member for steering.

This design was an offshoot of our wagon racing days. More stable than a wagon, it was faster. Well, it seemed faster anyway. Because we sat lower, I suppose we felt like we were going faster, yet we were still no swifter than the person we compelled to push us.

My next step up the transportation ladder was a bicycle. And step up it was, for a young boy, bicycles were very important. Like a status symbol, they showed you were growing up, becoming more independent. A boy on a bike could travel far and fast and more importantly, out of the view and control of his parents.

Before I had my own bicycle, I relied on my sister's bike or walking, or a tandem ride with one of my friends, especially when there was much distance to travel.

"Hop on. I'll give you a ride," one might say. Riders then had three options, rear fender, handlebar, or the center bar between the seat post and handlebars.

The rear fender was for smaller kids, it wouldn't support much weight. The handlebars offered the advantage of allowing the rider to jump off quickly if necessary. But our usual method was sitting sidesaddle on the center bar. This was stable and balanced, but often left the rider with a numb leg or sore rear – or both.

After my parents realized I was getting too big to continue riding my sister's bicycle, they finally bought me my very own. No longer did I have to suffer the indignity of riding a "girl's bike." A 24-inch middleweight, it was a nice bicycle. Red and white, it had a sturdy frame, wide handlebars and coaster brakes, and it had a bracket on the front fender for carrying books or a lunch box – or a tackle-box.

"Now, I expect you to take good care of this," Mom said. "We can't afford to buy you a new bicycle every year."

And I did take care of it, washing it after every jaunt through grassy fields, oiling it after each venture through stream or mud. Yet somehow things fell off. First to go was the kickstand. Immediately after that, the chain guard, then the fenders. Before long, my bike looked like a stripped down hulk, a veritable portable pants leg-eating machine.

Perhaps it was the jumping over curbs or repeated tumbles over the edge of the sandpit that contributed to the damage. But it should have survived. I did.

In any case, the end was near. Coming home after dark one night, late for supper as usual, I left my bike lying in the driveway behind Dad's car. When Dad left for work the next morning, I heard a sickening crunch.

"Don! Come down here!" I don't remember much of that conversation, but I do remember becoming a walker afterward.

I continued to be a walker for the rest of that year, and through most of the next summer until my twelfth birthday. Then very unexpectedly, my father took me to look at brand new bicycles. I was excited. I envisioned myself, the wind rushing through my hair as I raced in a blur down the road to who knows where.

At the bicycle shop, Dad and I walked up and down rows of bikes as I tried to decide which one I wanted. Dad suggested an old-fashioned heavy framed bicycle with balloon tires, pointing out their superior strength and dependability. But I had my eyes on a racing bike, like Bill Wallace's. Bill had an English racer, a skinny-framed thing with narrow tires, three speeds and hand brakes. But I doubted Dad would permit me such extravagance. Then I spotted the one I wanted.

"There it is. That's the one," I said, pointing to a shiny English racer. To my surprise, Dad said, "You're sure? You'll take good care of this one."

"You bet I will," I said, overjoyed at the prospect of riding such a speedy bike as this.

"OK then. It's yours."

And that was that. No haggling. No pleading. No explanation. Nothing. Just, "OK."

I rode away from that shop smiling from ear to ear. Wait 'til my friends see me with this, I thought. Now I can really go places.

And for a while, I did take very good care of my new bike. I washed and waxed it every week, oiled the chain and wheel bearings, adjusted everything adjustable, checked each nut and bolt to make sure they were tight.

But soon I was back to riding in and out of town, along paths, over curbs, through woods and fields. I couldn't help it. My bike just had to go to those places.

We often rode to the Devil's Staircase at Riverside Park, following trails along the river, trails that were not designed for bikers but for hikers. The stone steps and steep hills were not only hard on our bikes but on us.

Once, while bouncing down a series of steps, I lost control and toppled over a ledge, landing in some small trees and brush above the water. Had the trees not stopped me, I would have landed in the river, but luckily, my bike absorbed most of the damage.

My friends and I took our bikes down the Black Bridge Road to the archery range and to the dump where we spent countless hours. Here too, our bicycles received their share of wear and tear.

By the next year its fenders were gone, the shifter was broken, and the brake cables had snapped. To stop, I had to place my foot between the frame and the rear wheel, pressing against the tire. This was effective, but hard on shoes. I still had a frame, two tires, handlebars and a seat, though the seat was loose. But that was good enough for me. Perhaps I should have seen the end coming, but I didn't.

One day while riding to visit a friend across the river, I rode down the Glen Street hill. Several blocks long, the Glen Street hill was always a source of thrills for boys. In my enthusiasm, I pedaled as fast as I could, going faster and faster. Exhilarated by the speed, my pedals were a blur as the wind blew through my hair. Tears spilled from my eyes and my tires hummed as I felt the thump, thump, thump of each crack in the pavement.

I was so enthralled by the speed, I failed to think about the highway at the bottom of the hill. By the time I realized the danger, it was too late. All I could do was try to make the turn.

Fortunately, I met no traffic. Unfortunately for my bike, a car was parked alongside the road in front of a home, directly in my path. I struck it squarely in the rear and was tossed up over the roof, rolling down atop the hood.

People inside the house heard the crash and ran out to see what had happened. They saw me getting to my feet and a man asked if I was all right. I lied and said I was and asked him to help me straighten my bike. The frame was bent with the front tire overlapping the rear.

He and I each took a wheel and pulled until the front tire cleared the frame. Then I quickly hopped on my bike and rode off to examine my scrapes and bruises in private.

I didn't realize the frame of my bicycle had cracked until later in the week when Schultzie and I were racing down the Black Bridge Road. My tires were fairly humming when suddenly my bike collapsed. One moment I was pedaling behind Schultzie, the next I was sliding on my belly, clutching the handlebars while the rest of my bike lay behind me. This ended my English racing bicycle, and I became a walker again.

Chapter 30
The Black Bridge Road

*S*omething as simple as a smell or a sound can flood my mind with memories, and I see once again the days of my youth as clearly as if they were happening at that moment. I wanted to share my memories with others so they might understand what life was like, at least for some.

However, some people might think that reminiscing like this is a waste of time. I know I did when I was young. But I have since learned that one cannot know how far you have come without knowing where you started. And unless you realize what was, you cannot hope to appreciate what is.

It is with a great appreciation for life that I have told these stories. They by no means provide a clear or complete picture of life then, just a brief snapshot of life, my life. Someone else would paint a completely different picture. And so, they should, for every person has a story to tell, each one interesting.

No boy could ever hope for a better place to grow up than I had. The perfect mix of families and friends, of activities, adventure and innocence made it so.

I remember the smell of creosote wafting on the breeze of a hot summer night as it entered my bedroom window, beckoning me. The sound of trains passing beneath the bridge carried on that same breeze, instilled in me a sense of wonder. The old bridge was built of huge creosote coated timbers and it spanned railroad tracks a half-mile down the road.

The Black Bridge Road itself was lined with massive, spreading elms that provided shade and shelter to many living things, not the least of which was we kids. I remember the summer I turned thirteen when the last of those beautiful elms was removed. Before those trees were dismembered and hauled away, their massive corpses furnished forts and castles and sea-going ships for us to play on, their huge, hollow trunks providing the perfect place for us to hide.

I played in a series of fields across the road from my home finding unlimited adventure. I hunted lions and tigers with spears of dried horseweed, threw dirt-clod hand-grenades, shot bow and arrows and B-B guns. There, along the Black Bridge Road, I ambled through my youth with few cares.

The gravel pit was another favorite place for us to play. Running and leaping over the edge, we fell 30, 40, even 50 feet, before landing on the steep sloping bank amid the loose gravel. Sliding or tumbling still farther, at last we stopped and began the arduous climb back up again.

With every scrambling step we took, we slid back nearly as far, the sand slipping from beneath our feet carrying us with it. One could imagine a giant trapdoor spider below, pulling the grains of sand away, pulling us back and into its hairy grasp. That thought alone gave me motivation to climb still harder until, at last, I reached the top, ready to leap over once again.

We enjoyed throwing rocks over the edge, watching them splash in the clear-water ponds below. We swam in those ponds too and fished. We played with model army trucks and tanks in the sand, throwing firecrackers at each other's battle lines blowing up each other's army in imaginary wars. Then at night we rebuilt our tanks and trucks, repeating our battles the next day, much like real generals do today.

Near the bridge, a culvert beneath the Black Bridge Road allowed water to drain from cornfields on the north side of the road to the south side and into the pit. On the south side, the culvert hung out above the sandpit. Just seeing it there only made me curious to see more. So, one day, alone, I crawled into it.

The culvert angled downward, slightly but steadily. I hadn't room enough to go on my hands-and-knees, so I had to crawl on my belly and elbows. I never gave a thought to bringing a flashlight, so once I was in a short distance, I couldn't see a thing and had to rely on feel alone.

The darkness was unlike anything I had ever experienced before. But as I crawled deeper into the black tunnel, I thought about a story I once read of an army officer taken prisoner by the Germans during the Second World War. He attempted to escape through a narrow tunnel no larger than this, but his was laboriously dug by hand. As he crawled through the tunnel, he sensed something in the dark and touched what he thought to be a bone. Feeling around, he discovered what felt like other bones scattered about. Quickly he realized what he was touching, and just as quickly he heard a sound – the sound of giant carnivorous rats scurrying toward him through the tunnel – then suddenly they were upon him...

I suddenly lost my desire to see the end of the culvert and tried to crawl back out. There was no room to turn around, so I had to crawl backwards, uphill. The confined space made going very difficult, and the corrugated surface of the metal culvert hurt my knees and elbows. I bumped my head. Cobwebs clung to my face. Finally, after what seemed an eternity, I escaped, dirty, frightened and tired.

Did I go home, clean up and change my ways after that? No. I set out to look for more adventure. And the Black Bridge Road led to many adventures. At the city dump, just across the bridge, we found an abundance of adventure. My friends and I spent many hours digging through the debris there, wheeling our Radio-Flier wagons home filled with treasures. I still recall the heavy metal machine Schultzie, and I found with all of its places to connect wires. When we plugged it in, it not only hummed magnificently, but it had the strongest electromagnet I had ever experienced. We had no idea what it was then, and I have no better idea today.

Beneath the huge wooden beams of the Black Bridge, freight trains hauled gravel from the sandpit on twin ribbons of steel. The trains provided excitement for us as we ran alongside the cars and hopped on for a ride. And more than a few times we met hoboes who tried to convince us to join them in their lives of adventure. But we had adventures enough without them.

Schultzie and I once found that by placing .22 shells on the tracks for the train to run over, as some people might put pennies down, the shells not only flattened, but they exploded with a bang. From this we graduated to detonating the shells with a rock, then with a hammer.

One day at the bridge, we demonstrated this trick to some boys we met from another neighborhood. I placed a cartridge on the road and hit it with a rock. BANG! It went off. I laid another down and hit it. It too went off. I followed that one with another and another and another, until one didn't go bang! It went thud! It had simply flattened. I hit it again and BANG! It exploded.

A piece of the cartridge hit me in the temple. I wasn't badly injured, but the wound bled profusely. And because I didn't carry a handkerchief, didn't own one in fact, one of the boys gave me his to press against the wound to help stem the flow of blood. I held it there for some while before the bleeding finally stopped. A small crescent cut was all that was visible.

That night I lay in bed with my hand cupped against my temple, holding the wound away from contact with the pillow, foolishly imagining that gravity might pull the metal fragment down and out of my head. It didn't.

I never told my parents about that adventure, and I still carry that piece of brass in my skull as a reminder. After that incident, Schultzie and I moved on to other things.

One of those things was building rockets. We often found unburned railroad flares beneath the bridge and cut them apart, mixing their contents with gunpowder obtained from shotgun shells. This mixture was our "rocket fuel." For the rocket bodies, we used copper tubing, sealing one end with a wooden-dowel nose cone. We filled the tubing with our chemical mixture then partially closed the rear end by squeezing the tubing with pliers to form a nozzle. A firecracker fuse completed the rocket. We had only to apply a match and a little distance to our rockets, some of which actually flew in one piece, though never very far. Usually, they just smoked and spurted flames, though one time something more happened.

At that time, Schultzie and I built a rocket that we felt was especially hopeful. However, when we tried to light it, nothing happened. Repeated tries netted the same results

Schultzie and I took the rocket to his basement where we attempted to learn what had gone wrong. There we tried several things, even putting a candle under the rear to see if we couldn't get it to fire.

When even that didn't work, in frustration he placed the candle directly beneath the center of the rocket while we stood, one on each side and watched.

Then it dawned on me. If the rocket fuel did ignite, it had nowhere to go. Quickly, I reached to pull the candle away, and in that very moment the rocket exploded with a tremendous roar.

Schultzie's basement was filled with smoke and dust particles. My hand was peppered with tiny specks of blood. Something in my shoulder burned, and when I reached, I pulled a jagged piece of copper tubing from my flesh. But, by some miracle, neither of us was badly injured.

Gunpowder seemed to be the primary ingredient for much of what we did. To obtain the powder we cut shotgun shells apart, removed the wadding, exposing the powder. Then we carefully lit the powder with a match, jumping back to watch it flare skyward. When the flame reached the bottom of the shell, the detonator exploded in a shower of sparks.

This was especially impressive at night when we lay in a ditch beside the road and touched the gunpowder off as cars passed. Even more impressive was the language we learned from motorists who stopped when they saw this display.

When camping out with my friends, we followed the Black Bridge Road almost every night. Sometimes we followed it into town, sometimes into the country. Many times, we followed it to the outdoor theater on highway 26. Still other times the road led us fishing or to the railroad tracks or to Camp Cheerio, a long-abandoned girl's camp. The Black Bridge Road led us to adventure no matter which way we took it. And we took it often.

The Black Bridge Road still passes our old home, changed little over the years, although the road has changed. Gone are the fields and the pheasants; new homes having sprung up like the tall weeds I used to play in. Gone is the dump with its treasures. And the sandpit, which became the city landfill, has long since been filled in by "progress". Even the old bridge that gave the road its name is gone now. Today the neighborhood boys have to find a new route to adventure.

I'm glad I lived when I did, where I did, finding adventure in a simple clod of dirt or in a horseweed spear. I'm afraid life has become too fast and complex for boys to ever again experience the adventure we knew. Although with a little luck and imagination, they might still experience their own Black Bridge Road.

Don't miss out!

Visit the website below and you can sign up to receive emails whenever Don Allison publishes a new book. There's no charge and no obligation.

https://books2read.com/r/B-A-OETV-TPEDC

BOOKS 2 READ

Connecting independent readers to independent writers.

Also by Don Allison

Charlie
The Black Bridge Road

About the Author

Don Allison is a retired industrial process coordinator who left the work force to begin life anew. That life included writing, publishing, and television production.

He is the author of 2 other books, *Charlie*, the true story of a man who went from farming to mining, to bootlegging, to Chicago, where he became a part of Al Capone's organization. From there, Charlie went to northern Wisconsin where he managed a retreat for the gang. His second book is *Walkers Hollow*, a small village where you meet Characters and enjoy adventures of may kinds.